SCOTT KNEW THIS WAS
NOT JUST A GATE THROUGH
THE WALL. . . .

The green glow began as a sparkle in the center of the metal rectangle. As it spread to consume the entire door in the pulsing glow, the stone wall began to vibrate.

Scott froze as the pulsating light suddenly began to condense into a whirlpool of green fog.

Now or never.

He jumped and was instantly swept into a swirling vortex of a murky green mist that seemed endless. He became aware of a warm, prickling sensation coursing through his arms and legs.

The tingling intensified, flooding his entire body. Certain that he was disintegrating into all his component molecules and that they would *not* be put back together again, Scott screamed.

ARE YOU AFRAID OF THE DARK?™ novels

The Tale of the Sinister Statues
The Tale of Cutter's Treasure
The Tale of the Restless House
The Tale of the Nightly Neighbors
The Tale of the Secret Mirror
The Tale of the Phantom School Bus
The Tale of the Ghost Riders
The Tale of the Deadly Diary
The Tale of the Virtual Nightmare
The Tale of the Curious Cat
The Tale of the Zero Hero
The Tale of the Shimmering Shell
The Tale of the Three Wishes
The Tale of the Campfire Vampires
The Tale of the Bad-Tempered Ghost
The Tale of the Souvenir Shop
The Tale of the Ghost Cruise
The Tale of the Pulsating Gate

Available from MINSTREL Books

THE TALE OF
THE PULSATING GATE

DIANA G. GALLAGHER

A
MINSTREL®
BOOK

Published by POCKET BOOKS
New York   London   Toronto   Sydney   Tokyo   Singapore

This book is a work of fiction. Names, characters, places and incidents are products of the author's imagination or are used fictitiously. Any resemblance to actual events or locales or persons living or dead is entirely coincidental.

A MINSTREL PAPERBACK *Original*

A Minstrel Book published by
POCKET BOOKS, a division of Simon & Schuster Inc.
1230 Avenue of the Americas, New York, NY 10020

ISBN: 0-671-01407-2

First Minstrel Books printing March 1998

10 9 8 7 6 5 4 3 2 1

Cover photo by Mark Garro

Printed in the U.S.A.

For Nathan Lutz,
good friend and neighbor,
who's perfectly happy on Ivy Street

With special thanks to
James P. Hogan
for introducing the author
to multiverse theory
and the fascinating discussions
that inspired this book

THE TALE OF
THE PULSATING GATE

Prologue: The Midnight Society

Welcome to another meeting of The Midnight Society. You picked the perfect night to join us around the fire. Okay, so maybe it's not exactly perfect. It's so humid my shirt is sticking to my back and the mosquitoes are mounting a major invasion of the woods, but it could be worse.

Which is sort of what my story is all about.

My name is Gary, and one thing I've learned is that no matter how bad things seem, they can always get worse. Sometimes, we just don't realize how good we've got it until something really awful happens and it's too late.

At fourteen, Scott Fong thought his life was a complete bust. Shy and more comfortable with his faceless contacts on the internet than with real people, Scott hadn't made any friends since his family

1

had moved to Larson two years ago. However, he was determined to jump right into the social scene once school started and he entered Larson High. Making friends was even more important now that his older sister had suddenly started treating him like he had some disgusting, contagious disease. He and Teresa had always been close, and the mysterious change in her attitude was just one more crushing blow. His father, who had been unemployed for months, had taken a job that would keep him out of the country for a year. Having to cancel their Labor Day camping trip was pretty disappointing and Scott missed his Dad, but that was nothing compared to the humiliation of being forced to live with his grandfather on the outskirts of town so his Mom could save on rent.

Scott's grandfather was the town joke. Frank Fong had been a successful electronics engineer until he had retired. Now he was just a crazy old coot who invented ridiculous and annoying contraptions when he wasn't busy working on the huge but totally useless stone wall in the backyard that everyone called "Fong's Folly."

Scott didn't know it, but that stone wall was going to change his life forever . . . and not necessarily for the better.

Submitted for the approval of The Midnight Society, I call this story . . . The Tale of the Pulsating Gate.

CHAPTER
1

"Hey! Scott! Wait up!"

Scott stopped, hesitated with a weary sigh, then turned as Julio Estanza ran toward him. After a disastrous first week at Larson High, Scott was not in the mood to make small talk with the short, new kid. Julio, however, didn't give him any choice. With a tall hedge lining the walk on the left and students streaming by on the right, Scott's path was blocked when Julio planted himself in front of him.

"So, Scott! It's Friday. We're free. Feel like hanging out around town for awhile?"

"Can't." Smiling tightly, Scott shrugged. He didn't want to be rude, but the last thing in the world he needed right now was to be seen hanging out with a boy who had already succeeded in being classified as a loser by the Larson in-crowd. Not if he ever wanted to change his image and become a more popular and prominent force on the high school scene. "I've got things to do at home."

"Right." Julio nodded. "Guess you want to get your homework done and out of the way so you can enjoy the weekend, huh?"

"Yeah." As the rush of students flowing by subsided, Scott eased past Julio.

Undaunted, Julio fell into step beside him. "I heard there's a party at John Delahunt's tonight. Kind of a back-to-school bash for the freshman class. You going?"

"I haven't decided," Scott fudged. The mention of John's party was just another dismal reminder of how much of an invisible person he had become. At lunch that day, Patsy Walsh and Donna Tripley had been sitting across the table from him, talking about the get-together as though he wasn't even there.

"John's asked everyone who's anyone to come," Patsy gushed.

"Yeah, but word's going around that it's for the whole freshman class." Donna frowned.

Patsy sighed. *"Well, it is—sort of."*

"I suppose that's only fair. But to be honest, it'll

be a real drag if John's house is overrun by a bunch of weirdos." Donna rolled her eyes and shuddered. "Like that scrawny, new guy, Julio. He is totally spaced."

"Yeah . . . but don't worry." Patsy laughed. "Would you have the nerve to crash a party at John Delahunt's if you weren't invited?"

"And be on the most-popular-boy-in-school's blacklist for the rest of my life?" Donna grinned. "I don't think so."

Scott's cheeks flamed at the memory. Both girls had actually smiled at him before they left to dump their trays and return to class. In retrospect, though, he had to wonder if being excluded wasn't his own fault rather than a deliberate snub on their part. He had made so many excuses and turned down so many invitations in junior high, everyone had stopped bothering to ask. If he wanted to break through the social barriers now, he had to make the first move.

And the perfect opportunity to do that was waiting for him just ahead by the outdoor basketball court. Patsy was talking with John Delahunt and Kathy Giovanni, a new girl from California. Friendly and outgoing, everyone at Larson High had liked her immediately.

Perfect except for one thing, Scott thought with annoyance. Totally spaced Julio was glued to his side.

5

"Me, neither." Julio sighed. "Granted, a party would be a great way to get to know some of the kids, but there's a 'worst science fiction movies ever made' marathon on cable tonight. Three of them are so obscure, *I* haven't even seen them."

"That's a tough choice, all right." Scott's choices were clear-cut. He couldn't get rid of Julio without hurting the boy's feelings, but he didn't have to be *seen* with him. Abruptly turning to the left, he ducked through the hedge to the faculty parking lot.

"I could tape them and watch them later, I guess." Julio didn't miss a beat as he plunged through the hedge on Scott's heels. "The movies, I mean."

"Uh-huh," Scott mumbled absently as he quickened his pace and plotted a new course of action. Chances were good that John and a lot of the other kids would stop by the Fast Break Cafe before going home. His older sister, Teresa, would probably be there, too. And maybe she'd decide it wasn't beneath her eleventh-grade dignity to acknowledge her lowly freshman brother. For reasons she stubbornly refused to explain, Teresa had been going out of her way to avoid *him* all week. But first he had to ditch Julio, graciously if possible.

"If you were going to John's party, then I

would, too. 'Cause then I'd at least know *somebody.*"

Great! Scott choked back a gasp. Julio didn't know it, but he wasn't exactly welcome at John's. For that matter, Scott didn't know if *he* was on Donna's weirdo list. He *was* sure that no one would toss the new boy out or anything, but if anyone found out that Julio had gone to the big, exclusive bash because of him—he could kiss his future prestigious social standing good-bye. As he was quickly learning, Julio wasn't just odd, he was amazingly annoying.

"We don't really know each other, Julio."

"No, not yet. But we will." Julio grinned brightly. "I think we probably have a lot in common."

Besides being social pariahs?

"Like what?" Scott blurted out the question without thinking, opening the door to the friendly and lengthy discussion he had wanted to avoid. When they reached the street, he decided against turning back toward town. Obviously immune to taking any hints that were less than brutally blunt, Julio would just follow. It would be easier and less awkward to head home first. Besides, it was Friday and most of the kids would hang at the Fast Break until dinnertime.

"Like—I bet you spend a lot of time in on-line chat rooms, don't you?"

7

"What makes you think so?"

"Just a hunch." Julio shrugged. "I never see you talking to anyone much at school, which fits the on-line profile. Most of the people I talk to in the science fiction and fantasy chat rooms are like that anyway."

Scott fumed. He wasn't just irritated because Julio had pegged him so easily, but because the boy was right. It was a lot easier pretending to be someone and something he wasn't in computer print than it was being himself in the real world.

"I bet you like science fiction, too," Julio said confidently.

"Actually, no," Scott answered curtly. "I don't." Much brighter than his shy personality and average grades indicated, he indulged in adult internet discussions on topics ranging from politics to sports to controversial environmental issues and participated in reality-based game scenarios. He had no desire to escape into a fictional realm of the fantastic and ultra-weird. If anything, he wished he could escape from the fantastic and ultra-weird aspects of his own life.

"Really? That's a surprise." Julio frowned. "How come?"

"Oh, I don't know. Maybe because your grandfather sounds like such a character. Like someone straight out of a Jules Verne novel or something."

Scott stiffened. Even though his grandfather

was the town laughingstock and a source of painful embarrassment, Scott loved him. So what if the old man spent all his time and money inventing bizarre gadgets whose functions remained as mysterious as Frank Fong himself? Scott flinched inwardly. His grandfather's eccentric activities shouldn't bother him, either, but they did, especially now that he was living in the old man's house and not on the other side of town. He was so afraid of being ridiculed, too, he never defended the old man when the cruel comments and jokes started flying. He just pretended he didn't hear.

"I didn't mean that in a bad way," Julio explained quickly. "Quite the opposite. Like that stone wall I've heard so much about."

Scott frowned, anticipating the scoffing remark that was certain to follow.

"What does it do?" Julio asked curiously without a hint of sarcasm.

"Do?" Scott blinked. "It doesn't *do* anything." Which was why everyone called the huge, stone structure Fong's Folly. Standing seven feet high, the wall was four feet wide and stretched a hundred feet across the backyard, separating the manicured lawn from the thick woods that surrounded the isolated property on the edge of town. A heavy, locked metal gate was recessed into the stones in the center. However, the wall just ended on both sides. It didn't keep anyone or anything in or out of the yard.

"Nobody spends two years building something that doesn't do anything," Julio insisted.

"Nobody except my grandfather."

"Are you sure?" Julio asked seriously.

That brought Scott up short. He had given up asking the old man what the wall was supposed to do a long time ago. The only answer he had ever gotten was a slight smile, a wink and a shrug. He suspected that his grandfather enjoyed making everyone think he was daft. And if that was the only reason he had built the wall, Scott really didn't want to know.

"That's my house over there." Diplomatically dropping the subject of the wall, Julio pointed. "Do you want to come in for awhile?"

"Not today. Thanks." Waving, Scott hurried on without giving Julio a chance to invite himself along. He went home instead of cutting back toward town. Suddenly, the prospect of going into the Fast Break and being ignored by his peers and his sister was too depressing to face. And he couldn't shake the uneasy feeling that the same thing might happen at the party if he showed up there, too.

Teresa was standing in the driveway when Scott

arrived. She had changed out of her good slacks and blouse into jeans, boots and a casual sweater. "Going somewhere?"

"If you must know, yes." Tossing her long, black hair over her shoulder, Teresa glanced at her watch. "Rusty Anderson is picking me up to go to the Fast Break."

"Mind if I hitch a ride?" Scott asked impulsively. If he went into the hangout with a couple of juniors, it might break the ice with the kids his own age.

"Yes, I mind!" Rolling her eyes, Teresa waved as a sporty, red convertible pulled in and screeched to a halt. "You really have to get a life, Scott. Your *own* life."

Stung, Scott watched her leave with a sickening sensation in the pit of his stomach. Like Julio, who had astutely guessed that he spent most of his free time sitting in front of a computer screen, Teresa's harsh words had struck a raw nerve.

He *didn't* have a life—not one that was worth living.

Racing toward the back door, Scott skidded to a halt. His grandfather was standing by the wall fifty yards away, oblivious to everything except the gizmos attached to the gate and his portable computer.

Suddenly, the gate pulsed with a greenish glow.

11

Scott froze with his hand on the doorknob and Julio's comment ringing in his ears.

Nobody spends two years building something that doesn't do anything. . . .

Obviously, Scott thought as his pounding heart subsided, *the wall does something, all right.*

The unsettling question was—what?

CHAPTER 2

Stepping into the kitchen that evening, Scott paused as his grandfather added water to the canned soup heating on the stove. The old man's neatly combed, white hair was still damp from a recent shower. Wearing blue denim coveralls and a clean, white T-shirt, he was dressed for another all-nighter in his basement workshop.

"What's for dinner?" Scott asked. Prone to working odd hours, his grandfather very often didn't eat with the rest of the family.

"Whatever you can find." Mr. Fong pointed to the pantry and glanced at the refrigerator, then calmly resumed stirring his soup.

Trying to take his mind off his troubles, Scott had spent two hours dashing off his math and geography homework and another two hours following an on-line discussion about advances in computer technology in the twenty-first century. He hadn't eaten since lunch and he was famished, but he wasn't in the mood for leftovers or whatever he could pry out of a can. "Where's Mom?"

"Visiting the Hathaways."

Sighing, Scott sank onto a kitchen chair and dropped his chin in his hands. He didn't begrudge his mother a night out with their old neighbors on Burrows Street. A month had gone by since his father had left to work on an industrial construction project in Australia and she needed someone to talk to besides her teenage children and a father-in-law who had very little to say or spoke in irritating riddles most of the time. Still, she could have left him something to eat. She always had when she was going out *before* they had moved.

"Soup?"

"No, thanks." Scott watched as his grandfather poured the steaming chicken broth into a large cup without spilling a drop, then spooned in the noodles without a single splash. He wanted to ask why the metal gate had started glowing earlier, but his train of thought was abruptly shifted to another track by the old man's next comment.

"That happened to me all the time, too."

14

"What?" Scott asked curiously. He had no idea what his grandfather was talking about.

Mr. Fong smiled sheepishly. "Being too nervous to eat before a party."

"How did you find out about that?" Scott gasped. Although his grandfather usually didn't say much, he always seemed to *know* everything.

"Teresa told me before she went to the movies." Picking up the cup and a package of crackers, the old man headed for the basement door. "Have fun."

Scott just nodded. There was no need to admit he had decided not to go to John Delahunt's. His grandfather would eat his soup and take a nap on the old sofa downstairs. When he woke up in an hour, he'd start working. The routine was always the same and once he locked himself in the cellar, the old man wouldn't think about anything except his projects. Scott wouldn't lie if his grandfather asked about the party tomorrow, but right now he didn't want to listen to another well-meaning but totally off-base lecture about how he was a social outcast because that's what he wanted to be. And *that* assumption was based on the ridiculous theory that everyone creates their own reality because reality was simply a matter of individual perception.

Reality can be molded into anything you wish— if you're willing to take risks and make the effort.

15

Not hardly, Scott thought, recalling his grandfather's words when he had complained about being lonely and bored right after they had moved in. He had been trying to change his reality all week and his efforts had gotten him absolutely nowhere. Ignored by his peers, deserted by his father, rejected by his sister, neglected by his mother and totally misunderstood by his grandfather, his reality was just getting progressively worse!

Indulging in self-pity wasn't accomplishing anything, though. It just made him feel worse about circumstances he couldn't control. Grabbing a handful of chocolate chip cookies, a can of soda and a flashlight, Scott went outside. It would be dark soon, but taking a brisk walk was more appealing than sitting in an empty house being constantly reminded that his mother and sister had things to do, places to go and people to see or that his grandfather *liked* being a hermit.

Sitting on the porch steps to devour the cookies and soda, Scott briefly considered walking toward town instead of through the woods. There was nothing stopping him from going to the party— except a nagging sense of dread.

What if he went and John wouldn't let him in? Or what if he got in but no one talked to him? Or worse!

16

What if Julio decided to go and then spent the whole night talking to him!

Scott groaned. In spite of his fanatical interest in science fiction, Julio seemed nice enough, but Scott's opinion of the new kid didn't count. If his social status was more secure it might be different, but as things stood now, staying home was definitely wiser than courting almost certain disaster. Besides, there was no way that many kids could get together in one place without someone having something insulting to say about the stupid wall.

Setting the empty soda can inside the screen door so he wouldn't forget to put it in the recycling bin, Scott stood up and shoved the flashlight into his back pocket. Then he ambled slowly toward the massive stone wall. In the gray light of the setting sun, the wall didn't look like a useless pile of stones. The contrasts of dark shadow and fading light across the uneven surface gave it a majestic and ominous quality he had never noticed before.

Maybe because he had never seen the heavy gate *glow* before!

Filled with an odd combination of curious anticipation and fear, Scott stopped in front of the metal barrier. Because he resented the embarrassment the wall caused him, he had never bothered to examine it up close. The gate was constructed of metal plates held in place by riveted metal strips. He was surprised to find that it didn't have a handle or knob, but an electronic lock with a magnetic key-card slot. Set in the meticulously crafted but primitive door that looked like it belonged in a medieval castle, the high-tech locking mechanism seemed totally out of place and unnecessary.

Except for that mysterious, greenish light.

Bracing himself, Scott placed his hand on the door. He wasn't sure what he expected, but all he felt was hard, cold metal that didn't pulse, glow or fry him in some exotic security booby trap.

Feeling totally foolish, Scott sighed. His eyes had obviously been playing tricks on him that afternoon. The gate hadn't glowed. It must have been open and the strange light had come from *inside* the wall, which measured seven feet high and four feet wide. There was plenty of room for a narrow corridor.

As he walked down the length of the wall toward the woods, Scott didn't wonder why his grandfather might want a hollow, stone wall in his backyard. Whatever the reason, it probably wouldn't make sense to anyone *except* Frank Fong.

"Scott?"

Hearing his grandfather call inside the house, Scott opened his mouth to answer, then hesitated. Only fifteen minutes had passed since the old man had gone downstairs to work. He wasn't taking his after-dinner nap, which was highly unusual for the dedicated inventor.

Through the kitchen window, Scott saw his grandfather disappear into the living room and heard him call again. Then he realized that the old man didn't want him. He was just checking to see if he had left for the party yet.

And *that* was even more unusual. His grandfather had an uncanny talent for being able to totally tune out everyone and everything when he was working or even just thinking about his projects. Scott was convinced the house could fall down around him and the old man wouldn't notice. And he doubted that his grandfather had more than a casual interest in his social life. Only one other explanation for the search and the old man's change in routine came to mind.

His grandfather was up to something that he didn't want anyone to see.

When the old man walked back through the kitchen and opened the screen door, Scott ran to the end of the wall. Hidden by stone and the darkening shadows, he watched his grandfather walk across the yard. When he reached the gate, he stopped and just stood, staring at the metal barrier with an expression of worried uncertainty. Intrigued and anxious for the old man to do something before it got too dark to see, Scott

19

stood perfectly still, too. Finally, his grandfather took a plastic card out of his pocket and stared at that.

The magnetic key?

Scott held his breath as the old man suddenly shoved the card toward the gate, then pulled it back and put it in his pocket. Hugging the end of the wall, Scott couldn't actually see the gate, but he assumed his grandfather had slipped the key-card in and out of the lock slot to activate it. A pulsing green glow lit up the side of the wall.

And the stones began to vibrate with a subtle rumble.

Scott jumped back with a startled gasp as the air suddenly became agitated, like it did right be-fore a major thunderstorm. Except, Scott realized as the hair on his neck and arms bristled, the charge was much stronger. Only a few seconds had passed since his attention had been diverted, but when Scott looked back toward the gate, the green light and his grandfather were gone!

Shivering with shocked surprise and a sudden chill as the air calmed and the stone wall stopped vibrating, Scott tried not to panic. His grandfather had obviously just stepped through the gate. More worried about the old man than getting caught spying, Scott switched on the flashlight and aimed the beam down the back side of the wall.

His grandfather wasn't there, so he had to be inside the hollow wall.

Doing what? Scott wondered as he jogged to the gate on the front side. He supposed it didn't matter if the old man was meditating, counting a secret fortune in gold coins or standing on his head—as long as he was all right. The gate, with its high-tech lock, looked exactly the same as it had before, and the metal was cold to the touch. It was also airtight. The green light inside the wall wasn't seeping through along the edges.

Scanning the wall with the flashlight beam, Scott assured himself that the tons of stone weren't in danger of caving in, either. His grandfather was eccentric, but he wasn't stupid. He had built the wall with such painstaking care and precision, it would still be standing when his grandson was an old man.

Taking a deep breath to settle his jangled nerves, Scott swung the flashlight beam down. As he turned back toward the house, he stopped suddenly and frowned. Something wasn't right.

Directing the beam onto the gate again, Scott froze.

The lock-slot was gone!

Fighting another surge of panic, Scott pounded on the gate. The gate was solid, but he ignored the painful sting that shot through his hand.

"Grandfather! Are you in there? What are you doing?"

Getting no answer, Scott raced to the end of the structure. Maybe the old man had rigged the lock so it could be removed from the inside. Except there wasn't a hole in the gate where it had been. Or maybe he had miscalculated and something had gone terribly wrong. As Scott dashed around the end and started up the far side, the stones began to rumble again and the air sizzled with the static charge. Stopping abruptly, Scott turned off the flashlight, then ducked into the woods. The gate had been activated again and this time he wanted a clear view.

Hiding behind a large tree, Scott choked back a cry of alarm as the metal gate *became* a greenish light that brightened and dimmed with the steady rhythm of a slowly beating heart.

His own heart was racing wildly as the pulsating light dissolved into a swirling green fog.

Then his grandfather stumbled out, clutched his chest and collapsed on the ground.

CHAPTER 3

Paralyzed by shock, Scott didn't react until the randomly swirling fog became a powerful whirlpool that vanished with a loud, sucking sound and a soft pop. The sudden reappearance of the solid metal gate broke through his stricken daze. Turning the flashlight back on, he ran to his fallen grandfather. The old man was struggling to his knees when Scott reached him.

"Grandfather! Are you all right?"

Mr. Fong's eyes widened in alarm and he spoke in a strained whisper as Scott took his arm. "Where—were you?"

Shining the flashlight on the old man, Scott gasped. His white hair was dirty and tangled and a purple bruise darkened his slightly wrinkled

23

forehead. The bib of his coveralls was caked with dirt and the front of his white T-shirt was shredded. His full face was now pale and gaunt and his expression betrayed an inner terror as he staggered to his feet. Clutching the key-card in a white-knuckled fist, he moved like every bone and muscle in his body ached.

"What happened?" Too overwhelmed to consider the gate's impossible transformations just yet, Scott focused on his grandfather's disturbing condition. He looked like he had fought his way through the interior of the wall!

"Where were you?" The old man repeated hoarsely.

"In the woods." Knowing that his grandfather had not wanted any witnesses when he tested the mysterious gate, Scott answered with a partial truth. He *had* been standing behind a tree on the edge of the forest. Since that response seemed to calm the shaken old man, he let it ride.

Nodding, the old man put his arm around Scott's shoulders. "Help me up to the house."

"Maybe you shouldn't move. You might be hurt worse than you think."

The old man sighed. "Only my scientific pride and arrogance have suffered any serious damage."

With an arm around his grandfather's waist, Scott helped him hobble down the length of the wall. Assured that the old man didn't have any

24

injuries worse than aches and pains, a bruised forehead and damaged pride, Scott's thoughts turned to the unbelievable nature of the gate. Unless he had been hallucinating, the metal door had changed into a light and then a fog. He didn't have a clue why, but one thing was certain: something terrible had happened to his grandfather inside the wall. Scott couldn't even begin to imagine what, and he couldn't ask the old man any direct questions without revealing that he had seen everything.

"What do you mean?" Scott asked cautiously.

"There are some things man was not meant to know."

Riddles again!

Cloaking his annoyance, Scott tried to think of another way to phrase his questions while they slowly made their way across the lawn.

Groaning as they stepped onto the porch, his grandfather gave him another opening. "I never believed that—until tonight."

"What?" Propping the screen door open, Scott stood back to let the old man go ahead. His foot kicked the empty soda can he had left on the floor, but he ignored it as it toppled and rolled under the table.

Mr. Fong paused in the kitchen to stare at the key-card he still held in his hand. After a moment, he sighed and shoved it into his back pocket.

"Believed what?" Scott prodded.

"I always thought proving a theory would be the ultimate scientific satisfaction. I was wrong." Sighing wearily, the old man shuffled toward the living room.

"What theory?" Since his grandfather had mentioned it first, Scott didn't see any harm in asking.

Looking back, Mr. Fong shrugged. "All things are when and where they should be. Good night."

"Uh—don't you want some tea?" Scott asked, desperate to keep the old man talking.

Mr. Fong shook his head. "No, but thanks. I've got a long day tomorrow and I'd better get some sleep."

"Why? What's happening tomorrow?"

"I'm going fishing with Tom Payne in the morning and then . . . I'm going to start dismantling the wall." The old man smiled impishly, yet sadly, too. "That should keep the local tongues wagging for another few months, don't you think?"

Stunned, Scott just blinked, then nodded.

"In the meantime," the old man said sternly, "stay away from it."

Knowing it was futile to press his grandfather for information he didn't want to give, Scott let him go without another word. Oddly, he would have been overjoyed to find out the old man was going to destroy the wall a few hours ago. Now he wasn't so sure.

Setting the flashlight on the counter by the soup pan his grandfather had neglected to rinse, Scott got another soda from the fridge and sat at the table to ponder the fantastic events he had seen— or thought he had seen.

Had the gate really become a light and a fog?

Or was it just an elaborate illusion?

Assuming that the transformation was real, what was the gate's purpose? What theory had his grandfather proven that was so disturbing the old man had decided to tear down the wall? And what did everything's place in the universe have to do with it?

Scott's head began to ache with frustration. Between what he had seen and his grandfather's vague references, he probably had all the clues he needed to solve the riddle. But he wasn't particularly interested in science and he couldn't put all the pieces together.

Right then he realized he knew someone who just might be able to make sense of the puzzle. Rushing to the phone on the kitchen wall, Scott dialed Information and asked for new listings. Two minutes later he was talking to a pleasantly surprised Julio Estanza.

"Hey, Scott! I sure didn't expect to hear from you tonight!"

"Yeah, well—uh, I was sitting here by myself 'cause everybody else is either out or asleep and I got to thinking about what we were talking about earlier." Scott winced. He sounded like a babbling dork!

Julio didn't notice or didn't care. "Like what? We talked about a lot of stuff."

Scott hesitated. He wanted to pick Julio's brain, but he didn't think it was wise to tell the boy what he had actually seen. He wasn't worried that Julio would laugh. Julio would believe him.

"Well, I was outside looking at my grandfather's wall and thinking about science fiction—"

"I'll be right over!" Julio cut in excitedly. "You live at the end of that dirt road off Route 20 across from Spencer's Orchard, right?"

"Yes, but—"

"See you in half an hour!"

Scott stared at the phone that had suddenly gone dead in his hand. He hadn't meant to invite Julio over. In fact, he *hadn't* invited him! The new kid was so starved for company, he had invited himself. But since it was dark and everyone who was anyone was at John Delahunt's house, Scott decided it wasn't a bad idea. Seeing the wall in person might inspire the science fiction expert.

Taking another soda out of the fridge, Scott picked up the one he had started, retrieved the flashlight and went to the front porch to wait. Twenty minutes later a breathless but eager Julio came jogging into the drive.

"This is so cool." Julio accepted the soda, then paused to catch his breath. "I gotta tell you. I've wanted to see this stone wall since I first heard about it."

"How come?"

"Like I said before, I don't think your grandfather would have built it just to give the town gossips something to talk about."

Scott couldn't help but smile. Julio's attitude was refreshing, even if he was a little pushy and talked too much. Taking the cue, Scott turned on the flashlight and led the way around the house. "Well, that's what started me thinking. If this was a science fiction movie, the wall would probably be something really far out, right?"

"Uh-huh."

Expecting a more enthusiastic reaction, Scott turned to find Julio lagging behind and glancing fearfully toward the woods. Like he was afraid of the dark or something.

"What's wrong?"

"That weird sound." Julio shivered. "Is that some kind of wild animal?"

Scott listened, but all he heard were the ordinary whistles, chirps and rustles of the nighttime forest. "No, it's just bugs and stuff."

"Oh. Sorry." Julio shrugged sheepishly. "This country living is kinda new to me. I can't go to sleep without the TV on because it's so quiet and it's taken me two weeks to get used to wandering around in the dark."

Scott started. "It didn't get dark where you lived before?"

"Yeah, but who noticed with all those city lights blazing away from dusk 'til dawn! Not that I ever went out much at night."

"Why not?" Scott asked, genuinely perplexed.

"Just too dangerous. I lived in a pretty rough neighborhood." Julio shrugged. "Guess that's why I got so interested in science fiction and started cruising the net. So I wouldn't be bored to death sitting around our apartment."

Knowing Julio had come from a large city explained a little about why he seemed so odd. Even if half of what Scott had seen on TV was true, getting along in a bustling metropolis had to be a lot different than living in a small town. No wonder the new boy was trying so hard to fit in. Too hard, Scott thought, but that wasn't his problem.

"Speaking of science fiction—"

"Right!" Closing the gap between them, Julio dogged Scott's heels as they hurried across the lawn.

Although Scott had never taken a close look at the notorious wall until that night, he had watched the construction from a distance since his grandfather had placed the foundation stones two years ago. Consequently, he had never experienced the overwhelming awe Julio felt when he saw it for the first time. The massive structure looked even more imposing and mysterious in the dark under the scanning flashlight beam than it did at twilight.

"It's fantastic!" After recovering from an initial, stunned silence, Julio cautiously touched the rough surface.

"Fantastic" didn't even begin to describe it, Scott thought as he moved toward the center. He gasped and stumbled as the light illuminated the metal plated door.

The lock was back on the front side!

"Why does it have a magnetic lock?" Julio asked.

"Good question." Nervously backing up a few feet, Scott sat on the ground and held the flashlight so the diffused beam hit the gate. "For that matter, why put a gate in a wall that doesn't enclose anything?"

"Unless it isn't just a metal gate." Stretching out beside him, Julio propped himself up on his elbows.

"Exactly what I was thinking. I mean, I know it's just a gate through the wall, but—" Scott sighed, choosing his words carefully. "What if the metal could, say—change into something else? A light or a fog or something."

"Like morph on a molecular level?" Julio gave Scott a curious, sidelong glance. "That's an interesting concept for someone who doesn't like science fiction."

"I watch TV and go to the movies. I'm just not heavily into that stuff like you are. That's why I'm asking you."

"Asking me what?" Julio paused uncertainly.

"For your expert opinion," Scott quickly explained. "If the gate could morph and had a purpose besides blocking a hole in the wall—what could it be?"

The animated enthusiasm instantly returned to Julio's demeanor. "Gosh! Let's see. What about a time portal?"

Scott sat back slightly. "So you could go forward or backward in time?"

"Yeah. Although in real life, given the way scientists *think* the space-time continuum works, it's probably possible to go forward—but not backward. But we're just speculating, right?"

"Right." Scott nodded, but his curiosity demanded clarification. "If they think we can go forward in time, why couldn't we go back?"

"It has to do with velocity," Julio said patiently. "I'm not sure of the exact computations, but if someone leaves Earth in a spaceship traveling close to the speed of light, the passage of time slows down on the ship. But time progresses normally on Earth. Follow me so far?"

Intrigued, Scott nodded again.

"So let's say a hundred years has gone by on Earth when the space guy gets back—but only *five* years have passed for him on the ship."

Scott blinked. "So he'd get back ninety-five years farther in the future then he actually lived?"

"Theoretically? Yes. It only works going forward, though. But we don't have to worry about that because we can imagine that your grandfather's gate can do anything we want it to!" Julio sat up and wrapped his arms around his knees. "Like go backward in time."

"Works for me." Before Scott could begin to explore the time portal theory, Julio proposed another.

"Or maybe it's a teleportation device."

"Maybe." Scott was familiar with that concept. However, the idea that his grandfather had invented a device that could reduce an object to molecules in one place, send the molecules through the air to another place and then put the object *back* together again seemed pretty far-fetched.

Then again, so did time travel.

But he couldn't ignore the fact that within the space of a few minutes, his grandfather had come through the gate in worse condition than when he went in.

Was it possible the old man had gone backward or forward in time and ended up in the middle of a violent event? Or had he teleported to some rugged, wilderness terrain where he had gotten the bruise and torn his shirt? Of course, it was entirely possible the old man had gotten hurt fumbling around inside the wall.

But that didn't explain the shifting lock.

All things are when and where they should be.

Scott was convinced the old man's puzzling statement before he had gone to bed held a major clue to the strange, pulsating gate's function.

When and where. Individually, those words could certainly apply to either time travel or teleportation, but maybe there was a different theory that related to both the temporal and spacial positions of a thing.

Scott prodded Julio again. "What about the idea that everything belongs in a specific time *and* place? Does that suggest anything to you?"

"Funny you should ask." Turning away from the gate to face Scott, Julio gazed at him intently.

Scott tensed under the boy's pointed scrutiny, wondering if Julio suspected his intense interest went far beyond mere speculation for fun. *Probably not,* he decided as Julio's dark eyes brightened.

"I was just thinking about another scientific theory that's pretty new, but totally fascinating. What if the gate is a portal into the multiverse?"

"The what?"

"The multiverse." Leaning forward, Julio tried to explain the complex concept. "Some of the world's most noted physicists think that the only way to explain certain inexplicable subatomic phenomena is if the universe has multiple layers. It's based on the premise that anything that can happen—does happen. Somewhere."

Scott blinked, bewildered but impressed with the range of Julio's scientific knowledge. Either the boy didn't limit his reading to novels or science fiction was a lot more interesting and diverse than he had always thought.

"Sort of like the pages of a book," Julio clarified. "Each page represents a progressive *phase* of reality in the multiverse. The theory is that each phase is slightly different than the ones before and after it, but—" Julio emphasized the 'but' "—the differences would become more and more drastic the farther someone got from the point of origin. From the phase where they started."

"Really?"

"Yeah!" Excited by the idea, Julio gestured wildly with his hands as he talked. "Like maybe in the phase right next to the one we're in now,

I *didn't* come over here because I decided to go to John Delahunt's party instead. *Everything* in that reality would be different because of that one little change."

"Hard to believe."

"It's just a theory." Julio shrugged. "But supposedly all time exists in the multiverse, too. And if that's true, a person *could* go backward! I can't quite picture how that would work, though. Maybe there's temporal layers within the spacial layers or something."

Scott stared at the gate.

When and where.

If there really was a multiverse and his grandfather had somehow invented a way to travel between phases, then maybe a better version of his life was waiting on the other side of the glowing green fog.

It would be easy enough to find out.

All he needed was the magnetic key-card.

CHAPTER 4

Another hour passed before Scott was able to break away from Julio. They had spent most of the time talking about the multiverse and exploring the endless possibilities the different phases might present. But as the minutes passed, Scott had found it harder and harder to concentrate.

"You're a million miles away, Scott." Julio's eyes narrowed with worry. "Did I say something to upset you? Or am I boring you to distraction?"

"No, not at all. I'm just really—tired. It's been a long day." Actually, he was totally preoccupied, but Scott couldn't tell Julio that without prompting questions he didn't want to answer. Although the discussion and Julio were both stimulating, they weren't nearly as intriguing as the plan forming in his mind.

37

"Yeah." Sighing, Julio got to his feet and brushed bits of dry grass off his jeans. "I'm kind of worn out myself and it's a long walk home. Maybe we should just call it a night."

Afraid that Julio had interpreted his pensive silence as a personal rejection, Scott walked him to the end of the driveway. He *was* anxious for Julio to leave, but only because his plan required immediate action and he didn't want Julio to know that he intended to activate the gate.

If the gate was just a gate in an ordinary stone wall, he'd look totally foolish if he told Julio he thought it really might be a time machine, a teleportation device or a doorway into another phase of reality.

But if the gate was any of those things, he wanted to experience it alone first. He'd decide whether or not to confide in Julio after he found out.

As Julio shuffled onto the dirt road, he hesitated and looked back. "I enjoyed talking to you, Scott. Let's get together again soon, okay?"

"Sure. Whenever." Immediately regretting his lukewarm response, Scott almost called Julio back. He checked the impulse with a resigned sigh. Julio would wait, but his window of opportunity to access the gate before his grandfather destroyed it was closing.

After Julio disappeared into the dark, Scott

rushed back into the house. Flicking on the kitchen light and setting the flashlight on the counter, he glanced at the time and was surprised to see that it was almost eleven. His mother and sister would be getting home soon, so he had to act quickly.

Taking off his shoes, Scott padded through the living room and up the stairs. The second-floor hall light was on as usual, which was a relief. He'd be able to see what he was doing—*if* he got that far unnoticed! The old boards in the steps creaked, and he had to stop several times to calm his racing heart. He wasn't just afraid of waking his sleeping grandfather. He felt guilty about sneaking into the old man's room to get the key-card out of the coveralls. He didn't have any choice, though. Considering the old man's warning to stay away from the wall, he obviously couldn't ask for the key-card and expect to get it. His only option was to *borrow* it for awhile.

When he finally reached the upstairs landing, Scott saw that his grandfather's door was ajar and paused. The only sound he heard was the gentle rumble of the old man's snoring. For the moment, luck was with him.

Tiptoeing across the hall, Scott peeked through the open door at the bed on the far side of the room. He swallowed a gasp as his grandfather suddenly turned over onto his back. The old man continued to snore, but Scott waited another minute to be sure he was still asleep. Although the coveralls were lying within easy reach on the floor, he didn't want to botch the operation just because he hadn't been cautious or patient enough to proceed slowly.

Taking a deep breath, Scott slowly pushed the door open wider and winced as the old hinges creaked. The old man didn't stir. Easing into the room, Scott reached the coveralls in three short strides, then squatted and carefully slipped his hand into the back pocket.

The key-card wasn't there!

Surprised, Scott froze for a second, then gently shook the coveralls and shirt his grandfather had discarded. The card didn't fall out of the folds, either. After running his hand over the floor and coming up empty, he stood up to quickly scan the dark room. The tops of the dresser and nightstand were bare except for an alarm clock, a few books and some personal items. No card.

A meticulous man in all things, his grandfather had put the key-card somewhere in the room for safekeeping.

And he had dumped his clothes on the floor instead of in the bathroom hamper! The totally neat and tidy old man was a *lot* more shaken up than Scott had realized.

Not daring to risk going through the drawers

40

while his grandfather slept, Scott quietly stepped to the door to leave. His disappointment was so great he almost didn't react in time when the front door opened and someone started up the stairs. Ducking back into the room, he held his breath as Teresa stepped onto the landing and went directly into her room across the hall.

Too close, Scott thought as he slipped through the door and padded back downstairs to the kitchen. Although he missed the late night talks he and Teresa used to have, he certainly didn't want to engage in a midnight discussion of why he had been snooping around in their grandfather's room!

Disappointed because of the missing key-card and unnerved by almost getting caught looking for it, Scott wasn't ready to go to sleep. The chocolate chip cookies had taken the edge off but now he was starving again. He also wasn't about to give up exploring whatever lay beyond or within the wall because he had run into a little glitch.

Monster glitch, he reminded himself as he opened the refrigerator and removed a plastic container filled with lunch meat and cheese. He had to find the key-card before his grandfather began dismantling the stone wall tomorrow afternoon. He'd just have to hope his mother and sister planned to go grocery shopping Saturday morning as usual so he could search the old man's room.

And hope his grandfather didn't take the key-card with him when he went fishing.

As he reached for a plate in the cupboard, Scott noticed the plastic dish drainer on the counter.

The cup and pan his grandfather had used for soup were both washed and had already dried in the rack.

Scott stared. The dirty soup pan had been sitting on the counter and the cup had not been in the kitchen when he had gone outside to wait for Julio two hours ago. His sister hadn't cleaned them because she had gone upstairs as soon as she had come home.

Which meant his grandfather had not gone right to bed! The old man had come back downstairs, brought the cup up from his workshop, then washed it and the pan.

And chances were he had stashed the key-card in his workshop while he was there. The old man was neat and orderly to the point of being compulsive. Since the key-card was an important piece of the gate project, it made perfect sense that he would put it somewhere in the cellar room devoted to his work.

Forgetting his grumbling stomach, Scott headed for the basement door.

And was immediately brought to another abrupt halt by Teresa's voice behind him.

"Where are you going, Scott?"

Suppressing the frustrated anger he felt at being thwarted again, Scott turned around. His sister frowned from the doorway, making him wonder if his face betrayed his nervous guilt. Teresa knew him better than anyone and could tell when something was wrong even when their mom couldn't.

"I—uh—need a screwdriver."

Teresa's glance flicked to the food he had left on the counter, then back again. "To make a sandwich?"

"No. To tighten the screws holding my computer desk together." Scott rolled his eyes and tried to sound exasperated. He ignored the disturbing fact that he was able to lie so easily. He and Teresa had always been totally honest with each other, but that was before she had decided he wasn't worth her time and trouble anymore.

"Then use this one." Teresa opened the junk drawer by the door and pulled out a household screwdriver. "Grandfather would have a fit if he knew you were rummaging through his stuff and taking his work tools."

"Yeah, I know. Thanks." Taking the screwdriver, Scott placed it on the counter and went back to making his sandwich. Wherever the keycard was hidden, it wasn't going anywhere until

43

his grandfather retrieved it or he found it. If necessary, he'd stay up all night to make sure he found it first.

"You didn't stay at the party very long." Helping herself to a cold soda, Teresa sat down at the table.

Feeling her hard stare on his back, Scott fumbled the bread from the top of the refrigerator. "I didn't go."

"Why not?" Teresa asked, sounding annoyed. "Just about everyone in the freshman class was going! It was the perfect chance to talk to people, make some friends."

Mystified by the degree of disgust in her tone, Scott looked back with a puzzled frown.

"You've really *got* to get a life, Scott." Shaking her head, Teresa averted her gaze to sip her soda.

Oh, I intend to. It just won't be here.

Fuming, Scott kept that thought to himself and countered defensively. "For your information, Julio Estanza came over here and we talked for over an hour. What do you care anyway? *You've* hardly spoken to me in over a month!"

"Well, you shouldn't be relying on me for company. There's a whole town full of kids your own age out there. Like Julio." Teresa looked up curiously. "So what did you talk about?"

"Just stuff. Nothing special." Scott couldn't mention their grandfather's mysterious encounter

44

with the wall or Julio's theories. Much more tolerant of the old man's bizarre inventions and reputation as a nut in the community than he was, Teresa would probably appreciate Julio's unprejudiced enthusiasm and acceptance, but he didn't want to arouse her suspicions. Smart as well as pretty, she'd soon figure out what he was planning, especially since she had caught him going down to the workshop.

Nothing was going to stop him from going through the gate.

"So is Julio as weird as I've heard or just a little eccentric like Grandfather Fong?"

"Hard to say." Scott shrugged. As much as he wanted to close the communication gap she had put between them, he didn't want to do it now! He finished making his sandwich in silence.

After a couple of minutes, Teresa walked out.

Relieved because she was gone, yet sad because he had let the opening pass, Scott put the meat and cheese away and poured himself a glass of milk. Although Teresa had gone to bed, he still had to wait until his mom got home and settled in for the night before he could resume his search for the key. Picking up his plate, he went into the living room. Watching TV would help him stay awake. Out of curiosity, he decided to tune in to the "worst science fiction movies ever made" marathon Julio had told him about.

Except Teresa was sprawled on the couch and a classic romantic comedy graced the TV screen in monotonous black and white.

"What are you doing, Teresa?"

"Waiting for Mom and watching a movie. Why?"

"No reason." Irritated, Scott just stood for a moment, holding his milk and sandwich.

Teresa glanced at him and frowned. "What's wrong? You're acting really strange tonight."

"Nothing's wrong. I was just thinking about a strategy for an on-line game I've been playing lately."

Stymied but not defeated, Scott turned toward the stairs to go to his room. He was too excited and anxious about whatever fate awaited him beyond the metal gate to pass the time watching an ancient, sappy movie or evading Teresa's probing questions. Sooner or later his sister and mother would go to bed. He'd just have to wait them out.

Then he'd find the missing key.

And if Julio's theory about the gate being a portal into the multiverse was right, maybe he wouldn't *have* an older sister to harass and frustrate him in the next phase!

CHAPTER 5

Scott woke up with a start slumped over his computer keyboard. Sitting up in his desk chair, he rubbed his aching neck and blinked the sleep from his eyes.

A colorful kaleidoscope pattern danced across the computer screen and the gray light of dawn flooded the room.

He had fallen asleep on-line!

Moving the mouse to clear the screen saver, Scott glanced at the game script scrolling by and the message in the lower-left box. His character in Ocean Trek, an entertaining and educational scenario that explored problems and solutions in the marine environment, had been reported lost at sea while on a water sample collection mission in a mini-sub off the coast of Africa—fate unknown.

Scott prepared to type in and send an S.O.S. so he wouldn't be totally deleted from play, then changed his mind. He didn't need to escape his dreary life in a computer simulation about concerned environmentalists versus greedy corporations and uncaring governments anymore. He was about to embark on a real adventure in his own backyard.

If he hadn't missed his chance to secure the key-card because he had dozed off!

Signing off, Scott glanced at the time on his desktop before he shut down the computer. 5:47 A.M. Maybe it wasn't too late.

Making as little noise as possible, Scott opened his bedroom door and crept into the hall. His mother and sister's doors were closed. Moving toward the stairs, he looked into the old man's room. His grandfather was still in bed, but he wouldn't be for long. On those rare occasions when he slept instead of working all night, he got up at six o'clock on the dot.

Today wouldn't be any different, Scott thought as he made his way downstairs. The old man would be getting breakfast in fifteen minutes even though Tom Payne wasn't picking him up to go fishing until nine. Since he had retired from his job as a breakfast chef at a busy hotel off the

Interstate, Tom refused to get out of bed earlier than eight o'clock for *any* reason.

Speeding through the living room into the kitchen, Scott didn't bother to turn on the lights. He grabbed the flashlight off the counter and went right to the basement door. He didn't want to turn any lights on in the cellar, either. If his grandfather came down before he finished his search and left the workshop, he could easily hide in the dark.

That, however, wasn't going to be necessary.

Panning the flashlight beam across the workbench in the center of the large room, Scott spotted the plastic key-card. The old man had just left it there in plain sight. As Scott picked it up, he felt a major surge of guilt. His grandfather hadn't hidden the key-card because he totally trusted everyone in the family to leave his things alone.

But the lure of the gate and a better life was stronger than Scott's anxiety about shattering his grandfather's trust in him.

After thinking about Julio's three theories for hours last night, he was fairly certain the gate led to the multiverse—if it went anywhere except through the wall. That was the only hypothesis that incorporated *both* time and space. And assuming that was so, in the next phase maybe everyone in town thought his grandfather was a genius and not a crazy, old fool. Even better, maybe his father hadn't lost his old job because the state had decided to go ahead with the construction of new Interstate overpasses instead of canceling the highway improvement project! In that case, they'd still be living on Burrows Street. And he might even be one of the most popular boys in the ninth grade!

Pocketing the key-card, Scott fled the basement and ran through the house and up the interior stairway to his room. The old man went into the bathroom five minutes later. As he listened to the sound of running water, Scott suddenly realized he might have made a grave error in judgment.

Tom Payne wasn't due to arrive for another three hours. What if his grandfather didn't go straight to the garage to get his fishing gear together after breakfast, as usual? What if he went down to his workshop first and discovered the key-card was missing?

Then this phase of the multiverse was suddenly going to become even more intolerable than it already was.

But there wasn't anything Scott could do about that now except wait—again.

After his grandfather went downstairs, Scott quickly changed into jeans and a white knit polo shirt and slipped into his new high-tops. Then he sat on his bed to watch the garage from his window. Twenty minutes later, the old man walked across the driveway and opened the large front door. Another fifteen minutes passed while he collected and placed everything he wanted to take on the lawn at the edge of the pavement. Then, to Scott's immense relief, he brought out a plastic stacking chair and sat down to bask in the early morning sun and tie flies.

Ten minutes later, his mother got up and went downstairs. Teresa went into the bathroom.

Scott stayed put and kept an eye on the old man. He didn't want to do anything that was out of the ordinary, and ordinarily, he never showed himself on a Saturday morning before eight. At eight-fifteen he went down to the kitchen to bluff his way through the morning until everyone was gone.

"You look a little tired this morning, Scott." Mrs. Fong frowned with concern as Scott sat down at the table opposite Teresa and poured a glass of o.j. from the pitcher. "Didn't you sleep well?"

"Just not long enough." Scott shrugged.

"On-line most of the night again?" His mother's worried frown changed to one of disapproval.

"Playing that game, I'll bet." Teresa looked at him pointedly.

"Yeah, but it's not one of those stupid heroic role-playing things," Scott explained with annoyance. He always defended his on-line activities

51

and didn't make an exception this morning. "I've learned a lot about why marine life is in danger and what we can do about it playing Ocean Trek."

"You spend far too much time on that computer." Sighing, Mrs. Fong got in the last word and dropped the subject. "Cereal or toast?"

"Toast." Downing his juice, Scott caught Teresa staring at him. "What?"

"Mom and I are going to a huge garage sale at the community center before we do the grocery shopping. Want to come?"

"Give me a break." Scott had never understood why people enjoyed looking at and buying other people's junk. Like his grandfather's gate, that was one of the great mysteries of the universe— or multiverse. Except that in less than an hour, he'd *know* what was inside the wall. The attraction of garage sales would forever remain an unsolved puzzle—probably in *all* the phases!

"Do you have other plans?" Scott's mother asked without glancing back, as she started to fix a brown-bag lunch for her father-in-law to take fishing.

"Is Julio coming over again?" Teresa pressed.

"Who's Julio?"

"Just a new kid in school, Mom," Scott said wearily. His solitary social situation was bad enough without everyone constantly pushing him to do something about it. He had tried, but it was obvious to him, if not to them, that *this* reality was not going to change for the better no matter what he did. Making friends with Julio certainly wasn't the answer.

"No. Julio's not coming over and no, I don't have plans. I just want to hang out here, okay?"

"Fine," Mrs. Fong said, turning to look at him. "And since you don't have any plans, would you mind mowing the lawn? As a favor to your grandfather and me. He looks so worn out this morning, I'm a little worried about him."

Scott just nodded.

He couldn't say so, but he had plans. And they didn't include mowing the lawn.

Scott parted the curtains on the living room window to watch as his mother and sister drove out of the driveway. His grandfather was standing by the side of the road with his tackle box and other fishing gear piled at his feet. Tom Payne was already ten minutes late, but Scott didn't have to worry about the old man interfering with his plans now. Infinitely patient, his grandfather would wait right there until Tom arrived.

And by then, I'll be long gone.

Going out the back door, Scott pulled the key-card from his pocket and strode toward the stone wall. In the light of day, the wall and gate didn't look nearly as strange and foreboding as they had last night. In fact, Scott thought as he looked back to make sure the house blocked his grandfather's view of the critical center section, if he hadn't seen the gate dissolve into a swirling green fog and felt the effects of the oddly charged atmosphere or heard the rumbling vibration in the stones, he probably wouldn't have given his grandfather's excursion through the structure a second thought.

Stopping in front of the metal-plated gate, Scott took a deep breath and gripped the plastic key. He had taken a lot of risks trying to find it and he was still in danger of ruining his grandfather's high regard for him if the old man found out. If the gate was only a gate, he had taken those chances for nothing.

But there was only one way to find out.

And no reason to prolong his experiment.

Scott's pulse and respiration quickened as he slid the key-card in and out of the lock slot with trembling fingers.

Within a split second he knew this was *not* just a gate through the wall.

The green glow began as a sparkle in the center of the metal rectangle. As it spread to consume the entire door in the pulsing glow, the stone wall began to vibrate. Feeling the crackle of the static charge in his hair, Scott tensed as more of his grandfather's words surfaced to warn him away.

There are some things man was not meant to know.

It wasn't too late to turn back.

Scott froze as the pulsating light suddenly began to condense into a whirlpool of green fog.

Now or never.

Scott *had* to know.

He jumped and was instantly swept into a swirling vortex of a murky green mist that seemed endless.

Too terrified to scream, he became aware of a warm, prickling sensation coursing through his arms and legs.

Or maybe it's a teleportation device. . . .

Scott had been so convinced Julio's multiverse theory was correct, he had stopped thinking about the other possibilities the boy had mentioned. What if the gate was a time machine or a molecular transportation mechanism?

Nor had he considered the possibility that his grandfather might have *done* something to himself in preparation before he stepped into the fog. Like take a pill or drink some special potion to make sure he survived the gate's effects intact.

Scott hadn't taken anything except orange juice and toast!

The tingling intensified, flooding his entire body.

Certain that he was disintegrating into all his component molecules and that they would *not* be put back together again, Scott screamed.

CHAPTER 6

The shrill sound of Scott's terror was cut off as he was thrown back through the fog. He landed on his feet on the front side of the wall under a clear, cloudless sky. Dizzy from being in the spinning vortex, he stumbled, almost losing his balance. He looked back just in time to see the dwindling whirlpool disappear with a *whoosh* and an anticlimactic popping sound. The metal gate with its electronic lock was instantly back in place.

Breathless and shaking with a fear-induced adrenalin rush, Scott bent over and put his hands on his knees to calm himself. No wonder his elderly grandfather had come through the gate bruised and on the verge of collapse. It had been a wild ride! But, he thought with a quick glance at the familiar house, the gate had shoved him right back where he started.

Or had it?

. . . each phase is slightly different than the ones before and after it. . . .

As Scott pondered Julio's explanation of how the multiverse was supposed to work, he heard the sound of a car motor starting and looked at the garage. His mother waved as she backed the car out and toward the street. Teresa ignored him.

Stunned, Scott straightened and stared.

His grandfather's fishing gear was still piled by the plastic stacking chair instead of by the road.

Both these things were almost, but not quite, the same as they were before he activated the gate. Scott gasped.

The wall *was* a portal to other phases of the multiverse!

And *he* was in the next phase over.

Maybe. Scott frowned, remembering other parts of his discussion with Julio.

. . . all time exists in the multiverse, too. And if that's true, a person could go backward!

Or maybe he had simply gone backward a few minutes in the same, old reality.

Then Scott noticed the lawnmower parked by the side of the garage. An open gas can was on the grass beside it. Neither one had been there when he had walked across the lawn to the wall, and he had only been in the grip of the swirling vortex for a minute or two. Not long enough for his grandfather to have gotten to the garage, pulled the lawnmower out and returned to the road to wait for Tom.

And the Fongs didn't have a garden behind the garage in his original reality, either. His breath caught in his throat as he gazed at the neatly tended rows of vegetables in the dirt patch behind *this* garage.

There was no doubt about it.

He had definitely shifted from one phase of the multiverse to another through his grandfather's gate.

"Scott!" The old man called sharply.

Grinning, Scott waved at his grandfather as he walked up the driveway. He would never think of him as a crazy, old fool again, and the next time some town clown made a joke about the wall—

"What do you think you're doing?" Mr. Fong snapped angrily. A scowl wrinkled his face. "Get your lazy bones over here."

Scott blinked. He had never seen the old man so angry or heard him speak in such a nasty tone before. His grandfather was always kind and had an exasperating way of sounding disappointed instead of mad whenever Scott did something wrong, which always made him feel guilty, which was far worse than getting yelled at.

But this wasn't his grandfather. Or rather, it was—but it wasn't. Not exactly.

"Now!" The old guy fumed as Scott started toward him. "I want the lawn mowed and the garden weeded before I get home."

"Yes, sir," Scott mumbled as he picked up the gas can. Confused and needing time to adjust to his slightly altered circumstances, he decided to play along. Tom Payne would be arriving any minute to take the old man away. Then he'd be alone to think.

"And don't you dare go back to sleep! Your work will get done and get done right whether you stay out half the night partying or not. Got it?"

Dumbfounded, Scott nodded. He had *gone* to John Delahunt's party in this phase! And since he hadn't come home until late, he must have had a good time. Suddenly, dealing with a cranky, demanding version of his grandfather didn't seem so bad.

"It'll get done right," Scott said evenly.

"It better. And another thing—" The old man shook his finger in Scott's face as he talked. "—don't go stomping around in the kitchen anymore when I'm taking my after-dinner nap! Between the racket you were making and indigestion, I had some pretty weird dreams."

Scott just nodded again. The man glaring at him

was so harsh and bitter compared to the grandfather he knew, he couldn't help but wonder why. The only things the two versions seemed to have in common were their evening naps and the stone wall with its metal-plated gate in the backyard.

"Can I ask you something?" Scott stammered nervously. "About the gate?"

"What about it?"

Ignoring the old man's obvious impatience, Scott plunged ahead. "What does it do?"

"Do?" Mr. Fong sneered. "Not a thing except fill up a hole in the wall. I *was* going to build a gateway to the infinite phases of reality, but I changed my mind."

"Why?" Scott asked, surprised.

"Because I wasn't about to invent something that might turn the narrow-minded jokers in this town loose on the rest of the multiverse, that's why!"

"Oh." Bracing himself, Scott asked one more, critical question. His real grandfather didn't care what the citizens of Larson said about him. In fact, finding out what a jerk he was in this phase might be *why* his grandfather had decided to destroy the gate and had warned Scott to stay away. It was possible this Frank Fong was lying about the gate's abilities to keep *his* grandson away. "Then why did you put a high-tech lock on it?"

"I didn't. Why would I lock a gate through a

61

wall that doesn't enclose anything?" Muttering to himself, the old man stomped toward his gear as Tom's pickup pulled into the drive.

While he waited for the two men to load the truck and leave, Scott finished filling the lawn-mower gas tank and thought about this new and intriguing information. If this Frank Fong hadn't invented a multiverse gate, then his real grandfa-ther's gate had been *totally* in control of the phase-shift. And since the *lock* had materialized with the gate when the green fog disappeared, Scott was sure the original, *working* gate had phase-shifted along with him.

Satisfied that he wasn't stuck in this reality with no way out, Scott turned his attention to other things. What had happened at the party here last night? Was the Scott in this phase more confi-dent? Or had a shy duplicate of himself decided to risk—

Scott's mouth fell open and his eyes widened as he reached for the gas cap dangling from the can.

What had happened to the Scott who usually lived in this phase when *he* entered?

The disturbing question hung over him like a dark cloud as Tom's pickup roared out of the drive.

Had the other Scott replaced him in his origi-nal reality?

Or had that Scott jumped into an entirely different phase, displacing yet another version of Scott Fong?

Maybe that explained why this Frank Fong had had weird dreams. He had been taking a nap when his real grandfather had entered this phase of the multiverse.

Tightening the cap on the gas can, Scott sagged against the garage wall. Just as he hadn't stopped to think whether or not there was some kind of necessary, life-saving prep required before entering the gate, he hadn't considered all the ramifications of his actions. Were *all* the Scott Fongs in existence shifting through countless phases of the multiverse?

. . . anything that can happen—does happen. . . .

Which meant that in some phase his parents had never gotten married and he had never been born!

The concept of infinite possibilities was too mind-boggling to comprehend. Hearing a girl's delighted laughter, Scott instantly focused on the distraction.

And almost fell over with yet another unexpected and stunning development.

John Delahunt and Kathy Giovanni were riding their bikes up the dirt road. In his own phase, John never even spoke to him unless it was necessary in class. Now he and the pretty, new girl from California were stopping by his house.

Scott hesitated, unsure of what to do. His other self *had* gone to the party and stayed late. Maybe his social status here was everything he had so desperately wanted it to be in his other life. Since all the evidence seemed to support this theory, he jogged down the driveway to greet them.

"Hey, John! Kathy! What's up?"

John stared at him, puzzled. Kathy looked from Scott, to John and back again.

Scott felt his confidence slip a notch under their bewildered scrutiny. He knew this phase's Scott had gone to the Delahunt house, but he *didn't* know what had happened there. Anxiously curious, he tried to act as though nothing was amiss.

"Great party last night, John."

"Oh, yeah?" John scoffed. "Then how come you stormed out half an hour after you got there?"

Scott felt the blood drain from his face. *Stormed* out?

"You really shouldn't be so over-sensitive, Scott," Kathy said. "So what if everyone makes fun of your grandfather's wall? *I* was so curious, I asked John to bring me out to see it. Is that it?"

"That's it. Fong's Folly." John grinned as Kathy looked past Scott to the stone wall that was just as notorious in this reality as it was in the other.

"It's, uh—big." Kathy nodded, then shrugged

with a questioning glance at Scott. "And your grandfather spent two years building it?"

Cheeks flaming with embarrassment, Scott just nodded.

"Stone by stone," John added. "The gate's a nice touch, don't you think, Kathy? Saves the old man from having to walk *around* the wall to get to the woods."

Kathy smiled uncertainly.

"So what's the old guy up to these days, Scott?" John asked. "Building a time machine in the basement?"

Scott resisted an impulse to tell them that the gate *was* a time machine of sorts and that he had just gone backward several minutes coming through it. Except that in this phase, his grandfather had never invented the mechanism. And they wouldn't believe him if he had anyway.

Kathy watched him intently for a moment, then shook her head. "You know something, Scott? If anyone insulted my grandfather to my face, I'd *do* something about it! You are such a loser."

Stunned, Scott stared at the girl as she nudged John and got back on her bike. Kathy hadn't rejected him because his grandfather was the town lunatic. She was thoroughly disgusted by his failure to defend him!

Ashamed and disgusted with himself, Scott watched them leave in devastated silence. The

Scott in this phase had botched the opportunity to improve his social position at the party, just as he had feared he would. And *he* had just botched the chance to win the popular new girl's respect and friendship! Now, Kathy would probably never speak to him again because she thought he was a spineless dork!

And he was.

In this version of Scott Fong's life, which was worse than the one he had left.

But he didn't have to stay in this phase!

Palming the key-card, Scott raced past the lawnmower to the wall. He activated the gate, then waited impatiently for the pulsating light to become the swirling green fog.

He hadn't gone to the party in his own phase. So the Kathy Giovanni *there* didn't know he was an over-sensitive, spineless dork. Leaping into the fog, Scott shut his eyes as the whirlpool grabbed him so he wouldn't get dizzy. Now that he knew Kathy might actually *like* him if he stood up for his grandfather, he could fix everything in his original life when he got back.

Opening his eyes the instant the gate spit him out, Scott muffled a cry of alarm.

Except he hadn't gone back!

CHAPTER 7

The frightening certainty that he had not landed back where he started was immediately apparent.

A dark cloud blotted out the sun.

And one end of the wall wasn't finished!

Shivering as a cold gust of wind whipped by, Scott snapped his gaze toward the gate to check for the electronic lock. Breathing easier when he saw it, he quickly surveyed the yard.

There was no sign of his grandfather's fishing gear. The lawnmower was parked in front of the garage and the grass had already been mowed. A weeding basket was overturned beside the vegetable garden. The Scott who inhabited this third phase had obviously been taken by surprise when the mysterious forces of the multiverse gate had somehow whisked him away.

And *he* had exited the portal more than an hour later than time in the last phase. That's how long it would have taken him to mow the huge yard and begin weeding. Except for the time difference and the weather, everything else seemed much the same as in phase number two. But he didn't know if the third Scott's behavior at the party and toward Kathy was identical, too.

If there had been a party and *if* Kathy had come out with John to see the gate.

Determined to find out on the off-chance that he had handled everything better here, Scott started toward the house. He could get Kathy's phone number from information. Since he could leave this phase behind, too, if necessary, he had nothing to lose by calling the girl. If she just laughed and hung up, it would be *this* Scott's problem when he got back.

Scott stopped abruptly halfway across the yard.

If he got back. He had foolishly assumed that the gate would automatically return him to his own phase. It had sent him on to somewhere and somewhen else instead.

Scott put that disturbing thought on hold when he saw Julio trudging down the dirt road.

. . . the differences would become more and more drastic the farther someone got from the point of origin. . . .

Since he was now two phases away from his

own reality, a lot of things could be very different. Maybe Julio was coming to visit because they had *agreed* to meet again this morning after talking last night! Which meant he hadn't gone to the party and totally ruined his chance at a friendship with Kathy! Or inadvertently rejected Julio because he was preoccupied with trying out the gate, either.

Scott ran to the end of the driveway to meet the new boy, but he wasn't at all prepared for the reception he got.

"Hey, Julio! Boy am I glad to see you!"

"Well, I'm *not* glad to see you, Fong!" Julio's dark eyes narrowed in a hostile glare.

Scott stared back in wide-eyed astonishment. Why was Julio so angry? Sagging, he realized there was an explanation that made sense given how the phases were progressing so far. Obviously, in this reality he had gone to the party after telling Julio he had decided not to. And Julio had found out.

"Look, if it's about the party—"

"Of course it's about the party!" Outraged, Julio threw up his arms. "It's hard enough being the new kid and trying to make a decent impression on everyone without having the number one *geek* in town talk your ear off most of the night!"

Appalled, Scott took a step back. This Julio was furious because *he* had latched onto him and made a pest of himself at the party. Exactly what he had been worried the Julio in his original phase was going to do to him! The amazing irony of the role-reversal was lost in the shock of finding out that other phase similarities had taken more drastic turns, too.

None of them for the better.

"I mean, whatever made you think I *wanted* to talk to you in the first place, huh?"

Numb, Scott just shrugged.

"Lucky for you my patience didn't run out before you did."

"I ran out?" Scott asked, then wished he hadn't.

"Yeah. Right after Kathy Giovanni called you a spineless dork for not standing up to John Delahunt when he insulted your grandfather."

Scott gasped. "She said that in front of everybody?"

Julio nodded with smug satisfaction. "Everybody who was at the party."

Which was most of the freshman class! Scott's knees buckled slightly as he pictured the humiliating scene. His grandfather was right. There were some things a person was better off not knowing. The results of going to the party were more disastrous here than in the second phase.

"But I've got to thank you for one thing, Scott."

"What?"

"*I* made a huge impression on Kathy. She thinks I was being tolerant and letting you hang with me because I didn't want to hurt your feelings."

"You? And Kathy?" Scott would have laughed if Julio hadn't looked ready to flatten him at the slightest excuse.

"Why *not* me and Kathy?" Julio's jaw flexed as he gritted his teeth.

"Uh—no reason." Raising his palms, Scott desperately tried to diffuse the boy's temper. Considering Kathy's attitude toward him because he hadn't defended his grandfather in the last phase, her attraction to Julio made a bizarre kind of sense. The new girl would appreciate his kindness toward an outcast, assuming her basic personality was the same here.

Julio's certainly wasn't. Growing up in a rough city neighborhood here had turned him into a mean and antagonistic punk instead of a weird, nice guy with a fanatic interest in science fiction.

"Gotta go, Fong. Do *not* talk to me again. Ever."

Not a problem, Scott thought as Julio turned away. He was going to get out of this phase and back to his own the minute Julio was out of sight.

Except he wasn't sure *how* to go back!

He knew it wasn't impossible because his

grandfather had gone through the gate and returned.

"Julio! Wait a minute!" Although he didn't really want to push his luck with this aggressive and surly version of Julio, it was a chance he had to take. Since the Frank Fong in this phase hadn't even bothered to finish the end of the wall, it didn't seem likely he had finished inventing the multiverse gate, either. Julio was the only person who might have a clue how to reverse the phase-shifting mechanism.

Julio spun to regard him coldly. "You're just begging for a black eye, Fong. Didn't I just tell you not to talk—"

Scott cut him off. "Just answer a couple of questions and then, I promise. Not another word ever. But right now, I really need your advice."

Julio shrugged. "All right. What?"

"You read a lot of science fiction, right?"

"Some. When I don't have anything better to do."

So far so good. Scott phrased his next question carefully. "Okay. If it was possible to shift between the different phases of the multiverse through a gate, but the process always moved you into phases that were farther and farther away from where you started—what would you have to do to reverse it so you could go back?"

"The multi-what?" Julio blinked, then frowned.

Scott's heart skipped a beat. Obviously, Julio was not only totally unfamiliar with multiverse theory, he thought Scott was putting him on.

"I'm out of here." Executing an abrupt about-face, Julio broke into a jog to put as much distance between himself and Scott as quickly as possible.

Spotting Tom Payne's pickup truck turning onto the dirt road off Route 20, Scott decided to make himself scarce in a hurry, too. Although it was too soon for Tom and his grandfather to be coming back from their fishing expedition in his own phase, there was no telling what the two old men were up to in this one. Maybe they hadn't even left yet, which meant his grandfather was still inside the house. Either way, Scott didn't have the energy for another confrontation with a more cantankerous version of the old man. Pulling the key-card out of his pocket, he ran for the gate.

As Scott waited for the door to cycle, he glanced at the storm clouds gathering in the western sky. And suddenly he was struck with an insight that made his blood run cold. He had phase-shifted twice and both times he had gone into a different reality, each one progressively *worse* than the last.

Shouldn't there be better phases of a person's reality?

There definitely were, he realized. Although he

hadn't been totally happy in his original life, it was a *lot* better than the lives of the Scotts he had displaced.

Knowing that the multiverse held better phases of his life bolstered Scott's sagging spirits, but didn't dispel the anxiety making his stomach churn.

If he went back, the phases would get progressively better, except he didn't know how to reverse the mechanism.

That wouldn't be a problem if the better phases were interspersed with the worse phases throughout the multiverse at random. Then he'd just have to continue shifting until he found a phase he liked.

Over the rumble of the vibrating stones he heard the pickup screech to a stop in front of the house. The green glow expanded to displace the gate, dimming and brightening with a steady, pulsing rhythm.

But what if the gate could only shift from bad to worse in one direction and from good to better in the opposite direction? If that was the case, he'd be better off staying in this phase until he figured out how to return to his point of origin.

Scott's mouth went dry and his skin tingled in the supercharged air around the wall as the whirlpool began to form.

"Scott!" Mr. Fong's angry voice boomed

through the eerie stillness that had settled in advance of the impending storm.

Framed in stone, the green vortex whirled and enlarged.

"How come you didn't finish weeding the garden, you lazy, good-for-nothing—" The rest of the old man's words were swallowed in a powerful gust of wind.

Scott glanced back. Most likely, this Frank Fong had also been taking a nap when his grandfather had displaced him. He didn't know the multiverse gate worked. But within seconds, the old man would clear the house and see him vanish into the swirling green fog.

Then the cranky old coot *would* know that another version of himself had succeeded in building a portal to the multiverse when he had failed.

And that might be enough to inspire him to try again.

Scott balked at the very idea. He would *not* be responsible for revealing his real grandfather's secret and unleashing even more chaos within the multiverse phases than he already had!

For better or worse—he jumped.

CHAPTER

8

It was worse.

And after completing three phase-shifts that had sent him into progressively more dismal realities, Scott was convinced that his grandfather had built a one-way gate.

And he was moving in the wrong direction.

Prepared to expect just about anything now, Scott sighed as he checked for the lock, then stepped away from the wall to look around. The sky was completely overcast and dark storm clouds were rolling in from the west. The lawn looked like it hadn't been mowed in weeks and the vegetable garden was completely overgrown with weeds. Apparently, the Frank Fong in this phase didn't expect him to do chores!

If there was a Frank Fong. Scott couldn't think about the pathetic and grouchy versions of the grandfather he knew as *his* grandfather anymore. And thinking about the endless *ifs* was giving him a headache.

Spotting the scattered rocks at both ends of the unfinished wall made the throbbing in his temples worse. What would happen if he phase-shifted into a reality where the wall didn't exist? Or he had never been born? Would he be stuck? Would he suddenly cease to exist?

Although those prospects were frightening, they also fortified his resolve to figure out how to go back where he belonged.

All things are when and where they should be.

Scott found some comfort in finally understanding what his grandfather had meant. Life in his proper phase of the multiverse wasn't perfect, but it was where he should be. After experiencing bits and pieces of the other Scotts' lives, he knew now that he was to blame for most of his problems. And those problems weren't nearly as awful as he had foolishly and selfishly thought.

Jamming the key-card and his hands in his pockets, Scott wandered toward the house. He noticed that the paint was peeling off the siding and one corner of the porch overhang had collapsed, but his mind was focused on other, more important matters. He felt really rotten for being so dissatisfied with a life that had actually been secure and full of promise.

His family honestly cared about him and wanted him to be happy. He even suspected that Teresa had stopped talking to him because she hoped that would force him to make some friends. Thinking back on the past week at school, Scott realized that he hadn't really tried to change how his peers related to him. He had expected *them* to *know* that he wanted to open the doors he had spent two years closing. Even worse, he had rejected Julio's friendly overtures because the other kids thought he was weird. Julio *was* weird, but he was also smart, pleasant and good company. If he had made friends with the new boy, then maybe everyone else would have accepted Julio, too. And if not, then at least he would have had one good friend, which was better than having no friends at all.

Lightning flashed in the western sky and thunder boomed, setting the ominous tone of the fourth phase and emphasizing Scott's unsettling reflections.

Most of all, he sincerely regretted how he had handled the town's ridicule of his brilliant and kind grandfather. He should have taken his cue about the wall from the old man's own attitude concerning the jokes. If *he* had just shrugged and smiled mysteriously whenever someone made a derogatory comment, maybe everyone would have stopped joking to wonder what the big secret was. If nothing else, he wouldn't have given everyone the impression he was ashamed and embarrassed by the old man. As hard as it was to admit it, he had been. And that more than anything made him feel like the spineless dork Kathy Giovanni had accused him of being.

But *not* in his original phase. Back there, Kathy hadn't even met him, yet.

It wasn't too late to change things for the better in his real life.

But first he had to find out *how* to get back to it.

Leaping over the broken first step, Scott jumped onto the back porch and paused. Since certain aspects of the previous realities hadn't changed much from phase to phase, his mother and sister were probably grocery shopping and his grandfather was out with Tom Payne. But he didn't know that for sure. Or even what time it was here.

However, given the unfinished condition of the stone wall, there was one thing he did know. Although this Frank Fong had apparently abandoned his multiverse gate project like the previous two versions, he *had* started it. And assuming all the Frank Fongs had some basic traits in common, Scott was pretty sure this elder Fong had taken and kept notes on the multiverse theory and the gate mechanism he planned to invent.

His grandfather knew how to reverse directions because he had done it. Scott was positive the answer was somewhere in those notes.

Hoping no one was home, Scott opened the screen door and slipped into the kitchen, which was just as neglected as the yard. The sink was piled high with dirty dishes and the floor was littered with trash that had fallen out of the overflowing container in the corner. The counter tops reeked of scum and dried garbage no one had bothered to wipe off.

"I'm leaving now, Teresa."

Scott froze at the sound of his mother's weary voice, then curiosity got the best of him. Moving quietly to the living room doorway, he peeked out and choked back a gasp.

His mom was wearing a waitressing outfit that looked similar to The Coffee Stop uniform back in his version of Larson. His *real* mother worked part-time as a teacher's aide in the elementary school to supplement the money his dad sent home from Australia. Mostly, she cooked and took care of their grandfather's house. Not only did this Laura Fong look ten years older, there was a hopeless sadness in her eyes as she regarded her daughter.

Who didn't look anything at all like *his* sister.

"I'm working a double shift today, Teresa."

Scott fumed as the overweight girl with tangled hair sitting on the worn sofa totally ignored her mother. Her T-shirt was stained and frayed at the collar and her jeans were worn through at the knees. Oddly, the sofa in this living room was the one his grandfather had in the basement workshop.

"I'd really appreciate it if you'd do the dishes."

Shoving a handful of popcorn in her mouth, the girl didn't speak or take her eyes off the TV.

Sighing with resignation, Mrs. Fong took her car keys out of her purse and left.

Reminding himself that this was not his family, Scott took a step backward and crunched a soda can under his heel. Panicking, he looked up as the slovenly Teresa snapped her head around. He wasn't surprised to see that her skin was covered with blemishes.

"What are you staring at, you little creep?"

Startled, Scott matched her narrowed, intolerant stare. The fear and frustration mounting within him because his adventure through the multiverse was not turning out at all like he expected fed the anger he felt toward the girl.

"Why don't you stop stuffing your face and do the dishes?"

"Why should I?" Teresa sneered.

"Because the whole house is a mess! I can't believe Mom let it go like this!"

"Like she has time for housework. Or cares. If you're so worried about her, how come you haven't taken an hour away from that stupid on-line fantasy game you're always playing to mow the lawn?" Teresa exhaled with disgust. "And where'd you get the money for the new clothes?"

Apparently, he wasn't a model son in this phase, either. Scott frowned and evaded the question about his wardrobe. "Why, uh—how come she's working a double shift?" He couldn't ask why his mother was working as a waitress at all. If he belonged to this phase, he would know.

"To pay the bills, dummy!" Rolling her eyes, Teresa picked up the remote and began flipping through channels.

"But isn't Dad—"

Teresa's harsh laugh cut him off. "What planet have you been living on? The jerk left us and ran off to South America last month, remember?"

"Yeah—" Scott hedged. "But—"

"There's no buts about it, Scott." Eyes flashing, Teresa lashed out. "He's gone and he's *not* coming back. The sooner you and Mom both accept that the better. I'm tired of listening to both of you whine about it!" She dismissed him by looking away and turning up the volume on the TV.

Crushed, Scott eased back into the kitchen and

slumped against the counter. He had felt totally betrayed when his real father had left for Australia. It wasn't just because the Labor Day weekend camping trip he had looked forward to all summer had been canceled. He had resented leaving Burrows Street to move into his grandfather's house. All of that was petty and unimportant compared to the tragedy that had affected this Fong family. *His* father had taken the overseas job so he could support his family and meet his responsibilities— not run away from them. And he would only be gone for a year. But like the Teresa and Scott in this phase and the other grandfathers he had met, this Ken Fong was a shabby imitation of the man Scott loved and missed so much.

And he was wasting valuable time!

Suddenly remembering something else that might prevent him from ever going home again, Scott rushed to the basement door.

His grandfather was going to dismantle the gate when he got back from fishing.

If he didn't return first—there wouldn't *be* a working gate to phase through!

"I wouldn't go down there if I were you." Teresa said matter-of-factly.

Scott hesitated with his hand on the doorknob and looked back to see her lounging against the doorjamb. "Why not?"

"Because the old crackpot has been acting even crazier than usual."

"Like how crazy?"

Opening the refrigerator door, Teresa pulled out a soda and popped the tab. Her manner softened slightly into a semblance of concern. "Last night after you left to go to the movies—"

"I went to the movies instead of to John Delahunt's party?"

"Why would you want to go to a party at that slimeball's house?" Teresa eyed him suspiciously. "Especially after what he did?"

Scott wanted to ask what, but didn't dare.

"Believe me, Scott. You're better off going to the movies alone than hanging out with that crowd."

Scott shrugged. "Right. What were you saying about Grandfather?"

"Oh, yeah." Taking a swig of the soda, Teresa wiped a dribble off her pudgy chin with her hand. "He like totally freaked. He came running down from his room raving about how some gate-thing works and how the whole universe is in danger of coming unraveled or something."

Uh-oh. Had this Frank Fong been *awake* instead of taking a nap like the other versions when he had been displaced?

"Personally," Teresa continued, "I think he had a nightmare about being homeless and living under an overpass in the city, but he thinks it really happened!"

Oops! Scott flinched. That answered that question. Although the other Scotts were also finding themselves rudely ripped from their known realities into progressively worse ones like this girl's grandfather, they would probably spend the rest of their lives believing they had just dreamed the experience. None of them had seen the gate activated or discussed it with Julio as he had. They didn't know about the multiverse and wouldn't even think about trying to build a gate. However, this Frank Fong might.

"I mean, he hasn't been all there—" Teresa touched her temple with her finger. "—since that gang attacked him and he fell off that stupid wall last fall."

Scott gasped. "Who attacked him? Why?"

"Helloo!" Teresa huffed with exasperation. "That Delahunt creep and his pals? Because everyone in town was so sure he was building some kind of doomsday machine? What is with you today anyway? Amnesia or what?"

"Nothing. Really," Scott said a bit too quickly. "So why shouldn't I go into the basement?"

"Because Grandfather's gone totally bonkers, that's why. He's been watching the wall through the basement window all night because he's convinced someone is going to appear out of nowhere and totally destroy life as we know it. He's nuts, Scott, and there's no telling what—"

Scott stumbled backward as the cellar door suddenly flew open and a deranged version of his grandfather grabbed his wrist.

"The key! Give me the key!"

Too paralyzed by shock to move or speak, Scott stared into the old man's wild eyes. The old man's grip was strong even though he looked more frail than the other Frank Fongs. His thinning, unkempt white hair stuck out at odd angles on his head, enhancing the demented expression on his gaunt face.

"Easy does it, Grandfather." Setting down the soda, Teresa cautiously approached. "Let Scott go."

"He's not Scott!" The old man's voice cracked with terrified desperation. "Not our Scott!"

"Granted, he's a little unhinged today," Teresa said evenly. "But it's Scott."

"No, it's not. You don't understand—"

"Come on, Grandfather," Teresa coaxed. "You haven't slept at all. Why don't you go up to your room and lie down—"

"No!" Mr. Fong wailed. "I can't go to sleep because I don't know where I'll wake up!"

Scott inhaled sharply as the old man's grip on his arm tightened and the wild eyes pleaded with the girl.

"We've got to get rid of the key! It's the only way to close the gate! To stop them!"

Scott paled. No matter what else happened, he couldn't lose the key. Without it, he had *no* chance of getting back where he belonged. Bigger and stronger than the stooped and broken man holding him, he yanked free and quickly backed away.

Shrieking, Mr. Fong lunged at him.

Teresa caught her grandfather around the waist and struggled to hang on. "Get out of here, Scott. Just until he calms down."

Scott didn't need to be told twice. He bolted out the door and raced for the wall.

Lightning cracked overhead and behind him he heard the table crash in the kitchen as Teresa tried to subdue the raving old man. The sound of the girl's high-pitched voice and Mr. Fong's hysterical screams mingled with the sound of rolling thunder. When the booming died down, he heard Teresa yell.

"Catch pneumonia! See if I care!"

The screen door slammed closed.

Still running, Scott looked back to see the old man stumble down the porch steps and fall on his face in the grass. Through the kitchen window, he saw Teresa go back into the living room. Since the old guy wasn't going to give up trying to get and destroy the key, Scott had no choice but to make his escape through the gate as quickly as possible. It didn't matter if this version of Frank Fong saw him disappear into the green fog or not. He really was crazy and no one would believe him.

Hoping he had enough of a head start to complete the transition before the old man recovered and caught up, Scott reached the gate and pulled the key-card out of his pocket just as the dark clouds unleashed a torrential rain. Unnerved by the crazy old man's pursuit and battered by the wind and pouring rain, Scott fumbled as he slipped the key in and out of the lock. Lightning hit a tree nearby with a deafening crack, severing a huge branch that crashed to the ground. Startled, Scott dropped the plastic card.

The stones began to vibrate and the speck of light at the center of the gate swelled into the green, pulsating glow.

As Scott leaned over to get the fallen card, the shrieking old man shoved him from behind. Sprawling in the slippery grass, Scott looked up as the wild-eyed Frank Fong picked up the key-card and laughed.

The hair on Scott's arms bristled with the static charge as the light transformed into a swirling whirlpool of green fog.

The gate was open.

Determined to close the multiverse portal forever, the old man drew back his arm to hurl the key-card into the vortex.

Scott's mind filled with one thought and one thought only as he scrambled to his feet.

If the key-card went through the gate and he didn't, he'd be a prisoner in this depressing phase for the rest of his life!

CHAPTER 9

Scott dove toward the swirling green fog as the old man threw the key-card into the gate. Mr. Fong's scream of defeated rage trailed off as he was snatched into the powerful grip of the vortex. When the gate flung him out with the same force as he had entered, he belly-flopped onto the slick, rain-soaked grass. The key-card landed in front of his dripping wet nose.

Closing his hand over the precious, plastic passport home, Scott stayed sprawled on the ground in a state of total emotional and physical collapse. His narrow escape from the fourth phase and the mad old man had been too close, and he wasn't at all anxious to discover what horrible differences this fifth phase presented. Although the storm had passed here, a cold wind whipped over him. His clothes were soggy from the rain in the previous reality and a damp chill seeped into his pores, adding to the misery of aching muscles and a homesick heart.

And he wasn't alone in his despair, either.

All the other Scotts were moving deeper and deeper into the darkening multiverse one phase ahead of him.

The last Mr. Fong's jump into a homeless life proved that.

Scott tensed.

Which meant that the Frank Fong in *this* phase was homeless and lived under an overpass in the city!

So where was the rest of the family?

Raising his head, Scott stared at the wet, brown grass he was lying on. As he struggled to his knees to scan the yard and house, his throat constricted with dread.

Brown tufts of dead grass dotted puddles of mud across the whole yard. Dead weeds drooped under the weight of rainwater in the vegetable garden. The porch roof had completely detached from the house on one side and creaked as it swayed in the wind. Some of the windows were broken. All of them were boarded up.

Scott held his breath, half-expecting to suddenly pop out of existence. Several seconds later, he realized that although the Fong family didn't live here, they existed somewhere in this darker phase. Maybe they were still on Burrows Street.

Gripping the key-card, Scott got to his feet and shivered. Not wanting to add to his misery by catching cold, he turned his back to the bitter, howling wind.

And froze in place to stare.

Filtered by the dark clouds, the light had an eerie, yellowish-gray cast that bathed the stones with a dim, ghostly sheen. But that surreal effect was not what had grabbed his horrified attention. This Frank Fong had finished significantly less of the wall than the others. And the portion that was still standing was in the process of caving in on itself and crushing the gate wedged in the center.

Scott had no way of knowing when the crumbling wall would finally collapse.

But he had to phase *back* before it did and the gate was destroyed. Considering the condition of the wall here, there might not *be* a wall in the next phase down the line. The strange charge in the atmosphere and the vibration in the stones when the gate was activated indicated that the wall itself was part of the multiverse mechanism and necessary to the shifting gate's emergence. Scott strongly suspected that without the stationary stone walls in each phase, the gate had nowhere to go.

Then would he spend eternity spinning in the sickening, green vortex?

Scott instantly shut that image out of his mind. It was just too horrendous to contemplate.

Chilled to the bone and to the core of his being, Scott headed for the back of the wall so the disintegrating barrier would block the wind. Since *his* grandfather's gate was controlling the entire process, he had to assume the other Scotts were still shifting ahead whether there were walls in those phases or not. Everyone shifted when he did and he wasn't too worried about getting them back where they belonged. Except he still had to figure out *how* to go back or they would all be lost.

As Scott scrambled over strewn rocks and around the jagged end of the stone barrier, he came to another, abrupt and stricken halt. Only this time, he hadn't been struck by surprise or fear, but by his own stupidity!

His grandfather had returned through the gate in the *back* of the wall!

Warmed inside by a ray of hope, Scott dashed down the length of the structure, leaping over piles of fallen rocks. However, his elation at finally having remembered the critical clue to reversing the gate's direction was instantly shattered.

There was no lock-slot on the back of the gate to pass the key-card through.

Overwhelmed with disappointment and exhausted, Scott sank to his knees on the wet ground. Behind him, the trees groaned as they bent in the wind. Overhead, a bolt of lightning split the dark sky and thunder roared in its wake. A loose board banged against the side of the house. Forcing himself to stay calm, Scott closed his eyes and tried to picture every detail of his grandfather's journey through the wall.

He had run to the gate after the old man and the green light had vanished. The lock was on the gate in front when he reached it, just as it had been on the front through all the shifts he had made. But the lock was *gone* when he glanced back after scanning the wall with his flashlight.

And it had switched sides *before* his grandfather came out.

Encouraged, Scott sat down, leaned against the wall and tried to think the problem through with the same logic his grandfather would have employed.

Since activating the gate from the front always moved him in the same direction going from bad to worse, it seemed reasonable to assume that the lock had to be switched to the back *before* entering the vortex in order to move from bad to better.

So how had his grandfather accomplished that?

Another insight suddenly surfaced—one that made Scott feel like an even bigger dunce for not having thought of it sooner. Although, he consoled himself, he probably would have in the last phase if he hadn't been so distracted by the family's deplorable situation and the crazy Frank Fong's determination to destroy the key-card. He had been on the right track when he had decided to consult the fourth Mr. Fong's notes.

His grandfather was as cautious as he was brilliant. He would not have gone into the multiverse without being reasonably certain he could return to his proper phase—which he had. In fact, since he was meticulous to the point of being compulsive, the old man had probably built *in* a reversing mechanism.

Scott didn't waste any time or energy berating himself for overlooking the obvious. Jumping to his feet, he immediately began examining the gate and the stones around it on the back side. The metal strips and plates on the gate didn't move or shift when he pushed, pulled, shoved and punched them. Nor could he find anything but stones, crumbling mortar and dirt in the wall around it. He was almost positive his grandfather would have installed a lock-switching lever or button or other device within arm's reach. Anything placed too far beyond the gate would be inefficient and dangerous in an emergency.

Suppressing a rising panic, Scott ran to the front, but after an intensive ten-minute search he had to admit that he was at a loss. It seemed totally out of sync with how his grandfather usually operated, but either there wasn't a lock-switching mechanism or the old man had placed it somewhere else in the wall. It would take him days to look into every nook and cranny and under every stone.

A large rock suddenly broke loose from the collapsing structure and fell to the ground several feet in front of him. Dirt and small bits of mortar clattered after it.

He didn't have days.

Shivering as the adrenalin levels triggered by his frantic search subsided, Scott turned into the wind to study the house. It had been deserted, not sold and occupied by someone else. Maybe this Frank Fong's equipment and notes were still in the basement workshop.

Energized in spite of a growing fatigue, Scott battled the howling wind as he hurried across the muddy yard. Kneeling on the wet ground, he rubbed the accumulated dirt off the cellar window and cupped his hands against the glass to peer inside.

The room was completely bare except for the center table, a bucket and a worn sponge mop.

Slamming his fist against the cinder block foundation, Scott rocked back on his heels and breathed in deeply until the pain ebbed away. The sting was oddly comforting and stimulated a stubborn will to persist he didn't know he had. Trapped in the multiverse on a one-way trip to apparent oblivion, he refused to give up.

He couldn't give up.

There *was* a way back.

But unlike his grandfather, who had designed and built the gate and understood the mysteries of the multiverse mechanism, he didn't have a clue what to do next.

And the Frank Fong in this phase wasn't around to ask. He was collecting discarded soda cans for spending money and sleeping in a cardboard box under a freeway.

But maybe Julio Estanza had just moved to Larson in this phase, too!

Jogging down the driveway, Scott spotted the faded 'For Sale' sign planted in the dirt where the front lawn used to grow. He dismissed it as irrelevant. Nothing in this ominous, dark phase mattered except the gate, the wall and Julio. He didn't care if this version of the boy was a sniveling coward or a belligerent bully. Regardless of the warped twists his personality might have taken, Julio was smart with an innate understanding of science and puzzles that Scott needed to tap.

When he reached Route 20 at the end of the dirt road, the next thing that supported Scott's suspicions that this phase was ten times worse than the one before was Spencer's Orchard. The trees were not laden with green leaves and bright red apples that would soon be ready to harvest. The bare branches looked like broken skeletons highlighted in putrid yellow against the dark, overcast sky.

Running down the highway toward town, Scott kept his eyes trained on the pothole-riddled road most of the way. He couldn't bear the sights that met his horrified gaze. Although some lawns and trees were still green and bits of color appeared here and there in windows and flower pots, there was a pervasive cast of brownish gray over everything. The wire field-fencing around Ned Johnson's small pasture was rusted. The paint on houses and stores was faded or peeling. Uprights were missing from porch railings and every car had a dull sheen. And the few people he encountered walked with stooped postures of defeat and kept their eyes averted in nervous fear.

As he trotted down the sidewalk into the main section of town, Scott couldn't shake the feeling that this Larson was steadily sinking into a state of decay that couldn't be stopped or reversed. He rejected the idea that the similarity to his own situation was a bad omen.

Slowing down to a breathless walk, Scott headed toward the house Julio had pointed out in a yesterday that seemed like a million years ago. Another surge of hope coursed through his tired body and mind when he saw the name *Estanza* printed on the mailbox. The drab house was badly in need of repair and no light shone through the dirty windows. However, with any kind of luck in this luck-forsaken phase, Julio would be home.

As Scott bounded onto the porch and raised his fist to knock, a hostile, sneering voice called out behind him.

"What hole did you crawl out of, Fong?"

"Out of some weirdo's closet, I'd say." A girl laughed. "And he obviously can't afford a decent haircut, either."

Scott turned and gasped.

John Delahunt, Kathy Giovanni, Patsy Walsh and several other kids from Larson High were standing on the sidewalk, glaring at him. Scott suspected that if *this* John Delahunt had had a party last night, the whole freshman class had *not* been invited. These kids were tough.

Everyone's hair, long and short, was teased into wild tufts around intricate cubic patterns where their scalps had been shaved. A jagged scar angled across John's cheek and he had a broken arrow tattooed on one of his square, bald spots. A lightning bolt in blue and red marred Kathy's pretty face. The boys were dressed in torn, stained T-shirts, jeans and leather or denim jackets studded with silver spikes. The girls favored long, black mesh tunics and patchwork vests over T-shirts and short skirts with ragged hems or tights. All of them wore scuffed boots and necklaces or earrings fashioned from twisted strands of steel and copper wire.

They looked like a band of rag-tag survivors as portrayed in every end-of-the-world movie Scott had ever seen. Considering the dismal deterioration that prevailed in their phase of the multiverse, their rough appearance and hostile attitudes seemed appropriate.

They were definitely dangerous.

And he was definitely not dressed to blend in.

"Too bad you didn't have the good sense to get lost and stay lost, dweeb!" John snarled.

Patsy smiled with malicious delight.

Kathy frowned and averted her gaze, clenching her lower lip in her teeth. She was not comfortable with the situation and afraid to say so.

Scott had a really bad feeling himself, but he couldn't let this crude and antagonistic version of

John Delahunt know how intimidated he felt. He glared back. "What's that supposed to mean?"

John shrugged as he repeatedly tossed and caught a large rock in his gloved hand. "You moved because your mother decided Larson wasn't safe for Fongs after we ran off that lunatic grandfather of yours, didn't you? You shouldn't have come back."

"Your grandpa never shoulda told anyone he was going to build a machine that would punch a hole in the universe, either," Patsy said.

"Yep." John sighed. "Crazy old Frank was so smart, he mighta done it. We couldn't let him finish that wall."

"We like the universe just the way it is." Patsy's smile faded into a menacing scowl.

"And it doesn't have *you* in it!" John heaved the rock.

Throwing his arms over his head, Scott ducked.

The last thing in the multiverse he had expected was to be stoned into oblivion on Julio Estanza's porch!

CHAPTER 10

Scott was even more surprised when he was suddenly grabbed by the arm, yanked off his feet and dragged through the front door into Julio's house!

As Scott stumbled across the carpet, Julio slammed the front door closed and locked it. A rock shattered a front window and landed on the threadbare carpet in a shower of splintered glass. The kids outside hooted and jeered and more rocks pelted the front of the house.

Regaining his balance, Scott saw a stack of dog-eared paperback science fiction novels on the coffee table. A definite plus. But as he turned to thank Julio, his words caught in his throat. Suddenly, he wasn't sure if he had just been rescued or dragged into even bigger trouble.

Wearing his own dark hair teased and swept off to one side, Julio had a skull tattooed on his bare scalp. A strand of wire was looped over his left ear. His black T-shirt was almost as worn as the carpet and there was a tear in the knee of his jeans. Hands planted on his hips, the boy glowered at Scott with dark, penetrating eyes that reflected the hard and bitter essence of the decaying phase.

"Are you really Scott Fong?"

"Yes." Scott answered simply. Something about the intensity of Julio's question put him on guard. He decided not to say *which* Scott Fong until he got a better handle on *this* Julio Estanza.

"The kid whose grandfather built that stone wall everyone in town calls 'Fong's Folly?' " Julio gave Scott a slow, studied once-over.

Scott nodded. He resisted the urge to flinch under Julio's curious glance, but he was very aware that his appearance didn't fit the norm in this phase. Even though his knit polo shirt, jeans and high-tops were wet and dirty and his damp hair was windblown into disarray, he wasn't wearing black or wire jewelry and not a single centimeter of his head was shaved.

"Did he really think he could do it?" Julio asked.

"What?" Scott tried to sound puzzled.

"Invent a way to get into other realities," Julio said matter-of-factly.

"Hardly." Uneasy with the questions, Scott evaded. Julio was just a little too interested in the wall and its potential function. Presenting him with a hypothetical problem about changing directions in the multiverse was probably not a good idea. He'd just have to figure out how to switch the lock himself. Right now, they both had a more immediate problem.

"You can't stay in there forever, Fong!" John Delahunt shouted. "Send him out, Julio, or you're gonna regret the day you came to this town!"

"We can always break the door down," someone else suggested.

With a quick glance over his shoulder, Julio motioned for Scott to follow as he headed toward the back of the house. "Come on. They'll just threaten to break in for awhile before they actually do it."

Although he didn't quite trust this Julio, Scott didn't want to be torn apart by a mob of berserk teenagers, either. He followed Julio through a small, dingy kitchen, then balked in the basement doorway.

Halfway down the steep flight of stairs, Julio looked back. "There's a way out down here. They won't see us leave."

Another living room window shattered.

On alert and wary, Scott hurried down into the gloomy cellar. One-on-one with a kid his own size, he had a chance of defending himself. He could handle Julio if he tried anything. But Julio wasn't looking for a fight. He darted over to a wooden door and opened it. "Through here."

Scott stared into the pitch-black darkness beyond the door. "What's this?"

Julio pulled a dangling string to turn on an overhead light, revealing a narrow passage lined with damp cinder blocks. "It leads to a bomb shelter. The people who used to live here built it just before the Soviets invaded Florida in 1963. There's another entrance on the far side."

The Soviets invaded Florida? Scott welcomed the darkness that hid his shock as Julio turned the light off and moved into the corridor, closing the wooden door behind them. He had been so caught up in how his own life was different in each phase, he hadn't really thought about dramatic changes in historical events. In *his* phase, the United States had forced the Soviet Union to remove their nuclear missiles from Cuba in 1962. Things had been pretty tense, but the Soviets had never even threatened to invade the United States and the two superpowers had not gone to war.

"Just keep your hands on the walls to guide you," Julio said. "There's nothing on the floor to trip over."

"Right." As they moved through the dark, Scott couldn't help but wonder about the Soviet invasion. Since Julio was speaking perfect English, he assumed the United States had won the conflict, but he was still curious. "I'm not really up on history. How long before we sent the Soviets packing back then?"

"Three days. My grandfather got his whole family out of Cuba and came to the States right after that."

"Yeah?" Feeling edgy in the dark, claustrophobic passage, Scott kept talking to steady his nerves. "I'm here because one of my ancestors came over from China to build the Union-Pacific Railroad 150 years ago."

Julio didn't respond right away. "Don't you mean the Omaha-Pacific Railroad?"

"Uh—yeah." Annoyed with himself for the slip, Scott shut up. In this phase, the first railroad through the west was named for the eastern starting point in Omaha, Nebraska. And this Julio had been sharp enough to catch his mistake. If he wasn't careful, the boy would quickly figure out that he was from some other *where* and *when*.

Warning Scott about another flight of steps, Julio led him up and out through a door set into the ground. The house blocked the line of sight from the front and none of the angry kids saw him and Julio slip through a tall gate in a rotting, wooden privacy fence. Safe in the alley that ran between houses, Scott relaxed a little—until Julio started asking questions again.

"Why did you come here anyway?"

Scott shrugged. "Just wanted to see my grandfather's old house again. He's, uh—missing, you know."

"I meant why did you come to *my* house?"

Good question, Scott thought, unsure of how to answer. Scott and Julio had never met in this phase because the Fongs had moved out of Larson before the Estanzas moved in!

"Your house was the closest when John noticed who I was. Sorry about the windows." A simple apology seemed lame under the circumstances, but Scott didn't know what else to say.

"Don't worry about it."

"Thanks. And thanks for the rescue, too." Smiling tightly, Scott started to back away. Just as everything else in this phase was rougher and darker than in previous versions, this Julio was more cynical and calculating than the Julio he knew. Although Scott appreciated the boy's efforts to help him, he couldn't shake the feeling that this Julio wanted something in return. Specifically, information about his grandfather's multiverse gate.

"I really gotta go, though, Julio. Before John

realizes we're gone and comes looking for me again."

"Where you going?"

Scott sighed. This Julio was annoying, too, but not because he talked too much. He didn't waste words going directly to the point. "Back to the old house. I can save an hour getting home if I cut through the woods."

"I'll go with you." A gleam of triumph lit up Julio's dark, brooding eyes. "I've been wanting to see that wall."

"Sure." Scott couldn't think of a logical reason to refuse. Even though he didn't want to wait to search the wall for the lock-switch, he could hang out in the woods until Julio left.

Eager to stay off the subject of his life in this phase, Scott tried to get Julio to talk about his. After several curt and totally uninformative answers to simple questions, he gave up and they walked the whole way back in silence. It was, however, no surprise when this Julio reacted to the unfinished and crumbling wall the same way *his* Julio had—with stunned awe.

"It's too bad the whole thing is falling down." Julio sighed, betraying a profound disappointment.

"He never finished it," Scott said pointedly. Although he didn't blame the boy for hoping to find a way out of this miserable existence, he knew that trying to escape into the multiverse wouldn't work.

"Because those brainless idiots ran him out of town." Frustrated, Julio kicked a loose stone lying on the ground.

Scott saw an opening to dispel any notions this Julio had about tampering with forces that should be left alone. "Yeah, but even before that, he had decided to abandon the project."

"How come?"

Scott held the boy's probing gaze with the most serious stare he could muster. "He was convinced that even if he could switch realities, he'd only be able to access worse phases—not better ones. He once told me that everything is when and where it should be. Crazy, huh?"

"Or brilliant. Seems to me that if you could go in one direction, you'd have to be able to go in the other direction, too. Maybe he just didn't develop his theories far enough."

"And maybe he did," Scott countered stubbornly. He used his Julio's example to prove his point. "I mean, that wouldn't be odd if you, uh—compare it to time dilation and the speed of light." This Julio knew exactly what he was talking about.

"You mean that time slows down for a person traveling away from Earth close to the speed of light?"

"Exactly. And when the traveller gets back, he's gone forward in time because more time has passed on Earth than it did for him. But—" He emphasized the 'but.' "—You can't go backward in time."

Unconvinced, Julio shrugged. "Maybe. Given physics as we know it."

"So maybe there's some reason a person could go to worse phases of the multiverse, but *not* better ones," Scott pressed.

"When they first invented cars, people thought they'd die if they went faster than sixty miles an hour."

Scott sighed. "Yeah and bumble bees can't fly."

"Aerodynamically speaking—they can't." Julio shrugged. "But they fly anyway. Sooner or later someone will figure out how to break the faster-than-light barrier, too."

Realizing that arguing with this equally intelligent and informed version of Julio was futile, Scott shut up again. Neither version was easily discouraged.

Easing up to the gate, Julio ran his hands over the smooth metal plates, then studied the electronic lock. "He sure built this gate to last, though. It looks—new."

Scott didn't know how to explain that, so he didn't say anything. Hoping that Julio would get bored and leave, he reviewed his grandfather's return from the gate again. Not only had the old man returned through the back of the gate, he had emerged with a bruise on his forehead, a torn T-shirt and dirty coveralls.

And suddenly those clues made sense. Scott glanced toward the top of the wall and inhaled sharply.

Julio snapped his head around. "What's wrong?"

"Uh—nothing." Scott took a deep breath to still the excited tremor in his voice. A thin strip of shredded white cloth was whipping in the wind on a jagged stone halfway up the wall above the gate. "Just anxious to get home."

And he *was* going home! The device to throw the lock from the front gate to the back gate was on the *top* of the wall between them. He couldn't see it, but he *knew* it was there. The white cloth was the vital clue he had been looking for. His grandfather had torn his T-shirt, bruised his forehead and gotten his coveralls dirty climbing the wall! Seeing the deserted house and the disintegrating condition of the wall in this phase had probably spooked the old man into finally turning back.

Scott could only guess why his grandfather had designed the system with the lock-switch in such a hard-to-reach place, but it was obvious he had to go over the wall from the front to make it

111

work. That's what the old man had done, even though it was a difficult climb for someone his age. Given the vibrations and the odd charge in the air when the gate was activated, it was possible the wall generated some kind of constant, low-energy electromagnetic field that was affected when a person moved through it to reach the switch. Scott didn't have a clue what that had to do with moving the lock from one gate to another and he didn't really care.

All he cared about was getting back to his proper place in the multiverse.

A rock whizzed by his head and slammed into the wall, barely missing Julio.

Both boys turned to face John Delahunt and his angry, violent followers as they marched across the muddy yard.

Scott immediately noticed that Kathy Giovanni wasn't with them. Then he remembered that she had not participated in the rock-throwing attack back at Julio's house. Even though she was wearing weird clothes and hanging out with John Delahunt's gang, she was, apparently, still a basically good person in this decaying phase. So maybe this Julio was, too.

Julio edged closer to Scott and whispered. "You'd better get out of here. Like now. I'll do what I can to hold them off and buy you some time."

Scott balked at running away and leaving the wiry but small new kid alone to fight his battle. And it *was* his battle. Even though none of the kids in his own phase had ever physically threatened or attacked him, he had never stood his ground against the jokes and derisive slurs they hurled at his grandfather. Neither had this Scott, but *he* had to draw the line somewhere and this *where* was as good a place as any.

"Seven against one? Forget it, Julio. I'm staying."

The mob halted ten yards away.

"Got your back against the wall, huh, Fong?" John laughed.

"Tell me something, Scott." Julio spoke softly and kept his calm gaze focused on John. "Are we friends where you come from?"

Scott started, then sagged in surrender. This Julio was too smart to be fooled into ignoring the slips he had made and the obvious differences in manner and dress that flagged him as a person who was totally out of place. Nothing he could say would convince the boy that he was the Scott Fong who belonged here. Besides, since his grandfather was going to dismantle the only working gate in the different phases, it really didn't matter if this Julio knew the truth.

"Yes, Julio. We are."

"Good." Julio smiled.

At least, Scott vowed as he returned the smile, they would be as soon as he got back and set things right with that Julio.

Fisting rocks they pulled out of the mud, John and his scowling companions began to advance.

If he *lived* long enough to get back.

CHAPTER 11

Setting his jaw, Scott caught a flying rock, dropped it and braced himself as two of the boys moved to flank him and Julio on both sides. For the moment, though, the hostile kids were all following John's lead and keeping their distance. John waited, glaring with a cruel grin and savoring the tension.

"Sorry, Scott, but you gotta go." Grabbing Scott by the arm again, Julio pulled him back to the gate.

"I can't just leave you, Julio!" Scott hissed.

"You don't have any choice!" Julio hissed back, his dark eyes flashing. "If something happens to *you* here and you *don't* leave, what happens to the Scott that's *supposed* to be here?"

Scott's eyes widened with understanding. Julio had confronted him with the one argument for leaving he couldn't ignore. The ultimate fate of all the other Scotts depended on him. He couldn't leave them trapped in more horrible phases.

"Okay. You win. But I've got to get to the back of the wall."

Nodding, Julio eyed the boys blocking Scott's escape around the ends of the barrier. "You'll have to go over the top."

Scott didn't argue with that. He *did* have to go over the top—and hope that the lock-switch wasn't too hard to find. As he put his foot in Julio's hands to get a boost over the gate, he looked the boy in the eye. "You're totally cool, Julio."

"Thanks. Maybe I'll try to find out where the *other* you moved when the Fongs left Larson. I could use a good friend." Julio faked an annoyed scowl. "But he won't be there to find if *you* don't get going!"

Grunting as Julio heaved, Scott got a handhold above the gate and hauled himself up. He scrambled over the rocks, then paused to look down one last time. "If you find him—tell him his grandfather's living under an overpass in the city."

Julio nodded. "Move!"

John Delahunt took that as his cue and began

116

to advance on Julio with a slow, deliberate stride. The four kids on either side of him matched his pace. The other two boys positioned themselves at the ends of the wall so they could move in on Scott regardless of where he came down.

Reaching the crest of the wall, Scott immediately spotted the digital glow coming from an electronic switch canted at an angle in a crevice. Like the gate, the high-tech switch apparently shifted through the different phases, too. An arrow pointing to the right on the device blinked in the faceplate beside a card slot. Pulling the plastic key from his pocket, Scott slid it in the direction the arrow indicated. The only effect he felt was a slight brush across his skin, like someone had run their hand over the tips of the hairs.

The visible effects were apparently more dramatic in the gate behind Julio. Scott listened as he cautiously made his way down the back side of the crumbling wall.

"What was that?" John Delahunt demanded.

"What?" Julio asked, then paused. "Well, what do you know? That gizmo just vanished into thin air!"

"Get Fong!" John shouted the order.

Although he was relieved to know the lock had shifted, Scott was all too aware that he might not have time to activate the gate and wait for it to cycle before the boys charging from the ends of the wall grabbed him. Landing on his feet before the back gate, he instantly slid the key-card through the slot, then shoved it deep into his pocket. He didn't want to risk losing it if he had to fight off the two boys.

As the pulsating green glow enlarged, the rumbling vibration swelled. The effect was amplified by the crumbling condition of the wall. Stones shook and rattled and the charge in the air was stronger than Scott had noticed in the other phases. Apparently, the wall wasn't just a housing for the multiverse mechanism. It served as a dampener for the electromagnetic field effects the activated mechanism produced, and the deteriorating wall wasn't working at peak efficiency.

The loud rumbling and visibly shaking wall brought John Delahunt and the four kids in front to a terrified halt. More loose stones rolled and bounced off the wall to the ground. The thunderous sound plus the pulsing green light sent the other two boys diving for cover in the woods.

"Run!" John Delahunt screamed. "That jerk is gonna blow this whole place apart!"

As Scott leaped into the foggy vortex, he heard Julio's fading voice call after him.

"Catch ya later, Scott!"

Closing his eyes to ward off dizziness, Scott braced himself for the chaotic situation he expected to encounter when he reentered the fourth phase. Landing square on his feet in a mud puddle, he was surprised to find the storm had passed. This crazy version of Frank Fong wasn't screaming on the front side of the wall anymore, either. He was babbling incoherently in an excited voice, apparently pushed over the edge into total insanity when Scott had vanished into the gate.

". . . gonna keep coming through here sending people on to living nightmares in times and places where they don't belong. Gotta stop 'em. Gotta blow up the wall—"

Teresa had apparently relented and come outside to get the old man. "No one's going to blow up anything, Grandfather. Especially you. I called Mom. We think maybe it's time you went to that nice resort we've been talking about. There's a lot of people your age living there. You'll like it."

Scott sighed as he pulled the key-card out of his pocket. At least he knew this Frank Fong would be properly taken care of in a nursing home. And as he suspected, no one was going to believe he saw his grandson disappear into a glowing green fog in the wall. Then, another familiar voice made him pause.

"Well, John wasn't kidding, Kathy." Julio shouted to be heard over the howling wind. "There really is a wall."

"What do you want, punks?" Teresa yelled.

"Just checking out 'Fong's Folly' for ourselves," Julio yelled back. "It doesn't look like much of a doomsday machine."

"Get lost!"

"Gonna blow it to smithereens!" The old man said.

Not daring to risk activating the gate in front of witnesses, Scott quietly moved to the end of the wall.

"No wonder Scott is such a wimp." In the driveway, Julio put his arm around Kathy and turned to leave. "His whole family is bonkers."

Kathy looked back over her shoulder and sighed.

The screen door slammed as Teresa took the babbling old man into the house.

Scott hurried back to the gate and inserted the key. This Julio was just as intolerant and tough as the one he had spoken to in phase three. But, Scott reminded himself, both Julios might have had a different attitude if those Scotts *hadn't* been such wimps.

Scott didn't know what to expect when he shifted back into the third phase. *That* Frank Fong had been rounding the house into the backyard when he had left.

The gathering storm was on the verge of breaking as Scott was ejected from the gate. A few drops of rain splattered his face as the vortex closed with a sudden *whoosh* and a *pop*. On the far side of the wall, he heard the old man call his name. A few seconds later the screen door banged closed. Scott immediately activated the gate to leave before the old man stormed back out of the house looking for him.

Scott only paused in phase two long enough to get the key from his pocket, slide it through the slot and return it to his pocket. As he spun in the violently whirling fog, he crossed his fingers. Unless he had miscalculated or the gate had suddenly decided to detour him to a totally different sequence of *wheres,* the next stop was home.

Stepping out of the gate, Scott paused to look up. The sky was clear, the air was still and the sun was warm. The gate closed with the familiar sucking and popping sounds—for the last time. He hoped.

Fairly certain he was back where he belonged, Scott took a deep breath and held it as a prickling sensation suddenly swept across his skin. Glancing back, he saw that the lock slot was gone and recalled that it had inexplicably appeared back on the front gate when his grandfather had returned, too. Apparently, the shift was automatic at the point of origin. Maybe because he had been right when he had tried to discourage the last Julio. Maybe there was some mysterious law of the multiverse that prevented anyone from accessing better phases.

If people could—they would. And the infinite but orderly structure of the multiverse would be thrown into total chaos.

He was also certain the Frank Fong in the next *better* phase either hadn't built a multiverse gate or, like his grandfather, had decided to destroy it. One thing he knew for sure—the Scott in that better life had not gone through the gate because *he* had never been displaced. *That* Scott had probably gone to John Delahunt's party and had a wonderful time.

He could only assume that the Scotts who had shifted with him had returned to their realities without being too traumatized by their experiences. They were probably just as glad to be home as he was.

Although *that* had not yet been confirmed.

Running to the east end of the wall, Scott cautiously looked toward the back of the garage.

No vegetable garden.

Confident he was back in his proper phase, Scott started to leave the cover of the wall. His heart jumped into his throat when he saw Tom Payne's pickup truck speeding down the dirt road—toward the house!

Ducking back, Scott tried to think clearly in spite of the panic gripping him. Tom and his grandfather had already left before he went through the gate the first time!

Then he remembered that they had returned an hour later in phase three. Besides, time didn't necessarily follow any set pattern in the shifts.

Even though his grandfather had cycled through four other phases and back again, only a few minutes had passed in this phase last night before he emerged from the gate.

Scott peeked out as the pickup screeched to a halt at the end of the driveway. Frank Fong got out and headed for the garage.

But *what* Frank Fong?

CHAPTER 12

"You're gettin' old, Frank!" Tom teased through the open truck window. "I can't believe you forgot your best reel!"

Good-naturedly waving the comment aside, Mr. Fong laughed.

His Frank Fong!

"Grandfather!" Overjoyed, Scott burst from behind the wall and ran to embrace the old man. "I've never been so glad to see anyone in my whole life!"

"I'm—touched." A puzzled frown creased Mr. Fong's forehead as he stepped back from his grandson.

Scott's initial elation at being home faded as he looked into the kind, questioning eyes. He had a

124

lot more to make up to his grandfather than his failure to defend the old man and his wall. Somehow, he had to salvage the broken trust the old man wasn't even aware of—yet. Pulling the "borrowed" key-card from his pocket, Scott held it out and stared at the ground while he confessed.

"I, uh—went through the gate in the wall."

"Really?" The old man's tone was calm as he took the card from Scott's hand. "Had yourself an interesting reality check today, did you?"

Looking up, Scott blinked. His grandfather didn't seem to be angry *or* disappointed in him. That *still* made him feel more guilty than getting yelled at like the second Mr. Fong had. It also prompted a desperate need to explain.

"I saw you go through the gate last night. I know I shouldn't have taken the key without asking and that you told me to stay away from the wall, but I—I thought my life might be better somewere else."

Nodding, Mr. Fong smiled. "I suppose it's human nature to think the grass is greener on the other side of the—" His gaze flicked to the massive stone structure. "—Wall."

"Maybe. But for me? The grass is green enough right here." Scott glanced at the lush lawn. "And this grass is way too long. Guess I'd better get busy and mow it."

"Yes, but I think the lawn will wait another day. Want to go fishing?"

Looking past his grandfather, Scott saw Julio trudging down the road. *His* Julio—who wasn't angry with him for making a pest of himself at John's party or thought he was a wimp or lived too many phases away, but liked him for who he was and just wanted to be friends.

"I'd love to go fishing, Grandfather—if my new friend Julio can come, too."

Whooping when Mr. Fong gave the okay, Scott ran down the drive. As he skidded to a halt and waved, an astonished but delighted Julio waved back. And Scott was struck by still another fascinating insight. In an odd sort of way, traveling through the multiverse *had* shifted him into a better reality.

Life in his proper phase would *get* better—because *he* was going to take the risks and make the effort to change it.

Epilogue: The Midnight Society

And it worked. Not only did Scott and Julio become best friends, the following Monday Scott introduced himself to Kathy Giovanni and invited her over to see his grandfather's infamous wall when she asked about it. Within a few weeks, he and Julio were hanging out at the Fast Break with the rest of the kids and they never missed another party. Scott wasn't even upset when Kathy and Julio started dating. Laura Kent moved into Larson the next spring and she and Scott hit it off right away. Laura thought the stone wall was totally cool, too. Mr. Fong had dismantled the multiverse mechanism in the gate, but he had changed his mind about tearing down the wall. As the old man so wisely put it, he had to pile the rocks somewhere!

Mr. Fong didn't have any reason to suspect that

the wall's existence might still be dangerous. Scott never told him all the details of his adventure, and the brilliant inventor didn't have a clue that Julio number five knew that the multiverse gate worked. Although he never located the fifth Scott or his missing grandfather, that Julio convinced his parents to buy the old Fong house. Three months later, he found Mr. Fong's multiverse research notes buried in the wall. John Delahunt and his friends had been so terrified the day Scott activated the gate, they never returned, and Julio was left alone to finish the wall and work on his improved version of the multiverse gate in peace.

Scott, on the other hand, never forgot that the fifth Julio knew about the gate, and the boy's parting words haunted his dreams. "Catch ya later, Scott!" Every once in a while, when Scott would find Julio watching him with a pleased, mysterious smile, he couldn't help but wonder what Julio he really was. He thought about looking for the skull tattoo under Julio's long dark hair, but he never did. If Julio number five had found his way into Scott's phase of the multiverse, then all the other Julios had gone on to better phases, too.

So tomorrow, when you're being driven crazy by itching mosquito bites, just remember that it could be worse. We could have been invaded by bees!

And with that thought in mind, I declare this meeting of The Midnight Society closed.

ABOUT THE AUTHOR

Diana G. Gallagher lives in Minnesota with her husband, Marty Burke, three dogs, three cats, and a cranky parrot. When she's not writing, she likes to read, walk the dogs, and look for cool stuff at garage sales for her grandsons, Jonathan, Alan, and Joseph.

Diana and Marty are musicians who perform traditional and original Irish and American folk music at coffeehouses and conventions around the country. Marty sings and plays the twelve-string guitar and banjo. In addition to singing backup harmonies, Diana plays rhythm guitar and a round Celtic drum called a *bodhran*.

A Hugo Award-winning artist, Diana is best known for her series *Woof: The House Dragon.* Her first adult novel, *The Alien Dark,* appeared in 1990. She and Marty coauthored *The Chance Factor,* a *Starfleet Academy Voyager* book. In addition to other *Star Trek* novels for intermediate readers, Diana has written many books in other series published by Minstrel Books, including *The Secret World of Alex Mack, Are you Afraid of the Dark?* and *The Mystery Files of Shelby Woo.* She is currently working on her next book.

What would you do
if you saw an alien...
in the mirror?

mindwarp™

For Ethan Rogers, Ashley Rose and Jack Raynes of Metier, Wisconsin, turning thirteen means much more than becoming a teenager. It means discovering they have amazing alien powers. Ethan is a skilled fighter—the ultimate warrior. Ashley can stay under water as long as she wants. Jack can speak and understand any language—human and otherwise.

They don't know why it happened, but someone does...and that someone or something wants them dead.

MINDWARP #1: ALIEN TERROR

MINDWARP #2: ALIEN BLOOD

MINDWARP #3: ALIEN SCREAM

MINDWARP #4: SECOND SIGHT

By Chris Archer

And look for more mindwarp novels, coming in 1998.

 A MINSTREL® BOOK

Published by Pocket Books

1429-02

NICKELODEON/MINSTREL BOOKS POINTS PROGRAM

Official Rules

1. **HOW TO COLLECT POINTS**: Points may be collected by purchasing books in the following series, *The Secret World of Alex Mack*™, *Are You Afraid of the Dark?*®, and *The Mystery Files of Shelby Woo*™. Only books in the series published March 1998 and after are eligible for program. Points can be redeemed for merchandise by completing the coupons (found in the back of the books) and mailing with a check or money order in the exact amount to cover postage and handling to Nickelodeon/Minstrel Points Program, P.O. Box 7777-G140, Mt. Prospect, IL 60056-7777. Each coupon is worth 5 points. Copies of coupons are not valid. Simon & Schuster is not responsible for lost, late, illegible, incomplete, stolen, postage-due, or misdirected mail.

2. **40 POINT MINIMUM**: Each redemption request must contain a minimum of 40 points, or 8 coupons, in order to redeem for merchandise. Limit one merchandise request per envelope: 8 coupons (40 points), 12 coupons (60 points), 15 coupons (75 points), or 20 coupons (100 points).

3. **ELIGIBILITY:** Open to legal residents of the United States (excluding Puerto Rico) and Canada (excluding Quebec) only. Void where taxed, licensed, restricted, or prohibited by law. Redemption requests from groups, clubs, or organizations will not be honored.

4. **DELIVERY:** Allow 6-8 weeks for delivery of merchandise.

5. **MERCHANDISE:** All merchandise is subject to availability and may be replaced with an item of merchandise of equal or greater value at the sole discretion of Simon & Schuster.

6. **ORDER DEADLINE:** All redemption requests must be received by January 31, 1999, or while supplies last. Offer may not be combined with any other promotional offer from Simon & Schuster. Employees and the immediate family members of such employees of Simon & Schuster, its parent company, subsidiaries, divisions and related companies and their respective agencies and agents are ineligible to participate.

COMPLETE THE COUPON AND MAIL TO
NICKELODEON/MINSTREL POINTS PROGRAM
P.O. BOX 7777-G140
MT. PROSPECT, IL 60056-7777

The Secret World of Alex

The Mystery Files of

Are You Afraid of the

NAME_____

ADDRESS_____

CITY _____ STATE _____ ZIP _____

THIS COUPON WORTH FIVE POINTS
Offer expires January 31, 1999

I have enclosed ___ coupons and a check/money order (in U.S. currency only) made payable to "Nickelodeon/Minstrel Books Points Program" to cover postage and handling.

❑ 8 coupons (+ $3.50 postage and handling) ❑ 15 coupons (+ $3.50 postage and handling)

❑ 12 coupons (+ $3.50 postage and handling) ❑ 20 coupons (+ $5.50 postage and handling)

1464(2of2)

Sometimes, it takes a kid to solve a good crime....

Original stories based on the hit Nickelodeon show!

To find out more about *The Mystery Files of Shelby Woo* or any other Nickelodeon show, visit Nickelodeon Online on America Online (Keyword: NICK) or send e-mail (NickMailDD@aol.com).

 A MINSTREL® BOOK

Published by Pocket Books

1338-04

THE HARDY BOYS® SERIES By Franklin W. Dixon